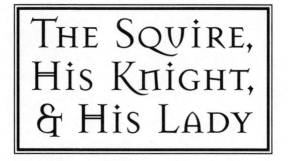

THE SQUIRE,
HIS KNIGHT,
& HIS LADY

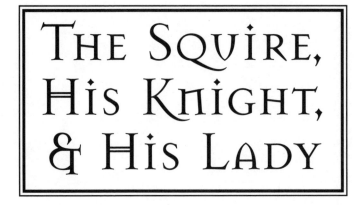

THE SQUIRE, HIS KNIGHT, & HIS LADY

GERALD MORRIS

Houghton Mifflin Company
Boston 1999

For Marilyn and for Denise —
whose lights only shine brighter

The text of this book is set in 12.5-point Horley Old Style.

Library of Congress Cataloging-in-Publication Data

Morris, Gerald, 1963–
The squire, his knight, and his lady / Gerald Morris.
p.   cm.
Sequel to The squire's tale.
Summary: After several years at King Arthur's court, Terence,
as Sir Gawain's squire and friend, accompanies him on a perilous
quest that tests all their skills and whose successful completion
could mean certain death for Gawain.
ISBN 0-395-91211-3
1. Gawain (Legendary character) — Juvenile fiction. [1. Gawain
(Legendary character) — Fiction. 2. Knights and knighthood —
Fiction. 3. Magic — Fiction. 4. England — Fiction.]   I. Title.
PZ7.M82785so   1999
[Fic] — dc21   98-28718   CIP   AC

Printed in the United States of America
BP   10 9 8 7 6 5 4 3 2 1

And therefore let me beg of you, my lords
If you should think my story ill accords
With the original...
Or if the words I use are not the same
As you have heard, I beg you not to blame
My variations; in my general sense
You won't find much by way of difference
Between the little treatise as it's known
And this, a merry story of my own.

—Geoffrey Chaucer

Contents

I	THE EMPEROR OF ROME	1
II	THE GREEN KNIGHT	24
III	SETTING OFF	44
IV	QUESTING	56
V	THE WILDERNESS OF WIRRAL	80
VI	THE ELFIN VILLAGE	107
VII	CHALLENGES IN THE NIGHT	124
VIII	BERCILAK'S KEEP	143
IX	THE GREEN CHAPEL	160
X	THE DUKE OF AVALON	173
XI	TO THE WORLD OF MEN	189
XII	THE GREATEST KNIGHT IN ENGLAND	210
	AUTHOR'S NOTE	230

I

THE EMPEROR OF ROME

Terence squinted down the shaft of a freshly carved arrow and twirled it in his fingers to make sure it was straight. It spun without a wobble, and he yawned and set it down alongside several other fresh arrows. Terence was bored. Whittling arrows and polishing armor was dull work for a squire who had seen as much adventure as Terence had. But King Arthur's wisdom as a ruler had brought peace to the land and left little occupation for the knights and squires who gathered at Arthur's court of Camelot.

In the center of the "Squire's Court"—an irregular open place between buildings, where the squires of Camelot met to brag and dream of the day when they would be knights themselves—several young squires hacked at each other with clumsy wooden practice swords. Sprawled in the shade at one side,

Terence watched them idly. Though he had no knightly ambitions himself, his years of service to King Arthur's nephew and greatest knight, Sir Gawain, had made Terence an expert critic of swordplay, and he could easily identify each squire's strengths and weaknesses. Mostly weaknesses, he thought.

One of the squires sparring in the courtyard, a fresh-faced youth no more than thirteen years old, separated from his opponent and turned to Terence. "Sir?" he said.

"Don't call me sir," Terence said.

"I'm sorry. Could you give me any pointers on my swordsmanship?"

"I noticed no swordsmanship," Terence replied, yawning. The boy flushed, and Terence relented. "All right. Come here." The boy stepped closer. "Hold your arm out in front of you — shoulder height," Terence said. "When your hand is over that line, your blade must be higher than your hand. Never, never parry a blow over that line with your hand higher than your blade."

"Did I do that?"

"Several times. And whatever were you doing when you spun around like that? I mean besides making a target of yourself."

The young squire grinned shyly. "I saw Sir Tor do it in the last tournament," he admitted.

2

"Sir Tor is an expert swordsman. You aren't. If you want to fight like Sir Tor, practice chopping at trees."

The boy looked hesitantly at Terence to see if he were joking, but Terence did not elaborate. It would take too long to tell of the time years before when he and Gawain had come upon the young Tor, then a sturdy plowboy, practicing with his sword in the forest and dreaming of knighthood. At last the boy said, "Yes, sir."

Terence closed his eyes and stretched. "Don't call me sir," he said.

Terence missed Tor, and missed even more Tor's squire, Plogrun the dwarf. Tor and Plogrun had been out questing for the past four months, and Terence was frankly bored with the younger squires. Across the court, a dainty boy in grey satin picked his way past a heap of garbage and chose a seat, which he carefully dusted with a handkerchief. "French," Terence thought, grinning. The other squires ignored him: continental knights and squires, with their sumptuous fashions and exaggerated graces, had grown common in Camelot. King Arthur had established treaties with several continental rulers. The most influential of these—the French King Ban of Benouic—was at Camelot at that moment on a state visit. This boy was probably one of King Ban's retinue.

"Terence!" Hearing Gawain's voice, Terence leaped to his feet. Gawain stood at the opening of the courtyard.

"Yes, milord?"

"Been looking for you. Work to do in the chambers, lad."

"What, today too?" Terence blinked.

"Guest of honor tonight, Terence," Gawain replied.

"You mean she's back? Already?" Gawain nodded, and Terence sighed. "I'll be right there." He gathered his arrows and followed Gawain. While at Camelot, Terence's squirely duties were few, but he had a few special responsibilities, having to do with the late-night drinking and arguing sessions that Gawain held with his friends. Terence had to prepare Gawain's chambers, serve the refreshments, and then help Gawain's friends back to their own chambers if necessary. Gawain had held one such session the night before, which was why Terence had been surprised, but Gawain had mentioned a guest of honor, and that meant that Morgan Le Fay was at Camelot.

Morgan was Gawain's aunt, the half-sister of King Arthur himself. She was also a sorceress, which did not endear her to Terence, but Gawain made his chambers available to her whenever she visited Camelot. Even though Terence did not trust Morgan, he had to admit that at times he felt an affinity with her. Earlier in their career, Terence and Gawain had gone on a quest for adventures and had found themselves in the Other World, a realm of faeries and magic. There, Gawain had fallen in love with a faery princess, and Terence had discovered that his own father was a ruler among the faeries. Now, though he and Gawain had returned to the World of Men years before, Terence had never lost the feeling that his true home was elsewhere. Morgan Le Fay, whatever else one might say about her, belonged to that Other World as well.

Terence passed by the kitchen court, and looked in. "Sophy!" he called.

"Hello, Terence!" a buxom girl called back. "Fancy meeting you here!" she said wryly. "What do you want this time?"

"Ah lass, I'm hurt, I am," Terence responded, in his best imitation of his master's native brogue. "Tha knows I've just come to see if ye're well, and ye accuse me of basely triflin' with ye!"

Sophy laughed and said, "And it's awful I'm feelin' about it, too. Now, tell me what you want, and keep your hands off the pastry."

Terence grinned. "Pastry? What kind?"

Sophy sighed. "Jam tarts. How many do you need?"

"It looks like a big one tonight. Lady Morgan's back. Three dozen tarts at least. How about meat? Any of that special chicken of yours — with the brandy sauce?"

"You're raving, Terence! Three dozen! And what about the king's table tonight?"

"He loved the flan you served last night," Terence said. "I heard him say so to the queen."

Sophy dimpled, pleased. "Well, I do have more flan," she admitted.

"You're a gem, Sophy. And the chicken?"

"No chicken, but we just got in a nice boar."

"A rare gem indeed," Terence said.

"Rogue," the girl replied, and Terence ducked out. He stopped again at the wine cellars and again at a springhouse, where the court's cheese was stored, before he arrived at Gawain's chambers. Gawain and Morgan were in the sitting room.

"Everything ready, Terence?" Gawain asked.

"Floor needs sweeping," Terence replied. "You can see Sir Lionel's outline in the dust there from last night. Is the king coming tonight, milord?"

Gawain said he didn't know, and Morgan said, "If he doesn't, then he should. Your 'little get-togethers' are the round table within the Round Table."

The king did come that night, but he didn't stay long. He drank a flagon of wine with Sir Kai, asked

Gawain how he managed to get fresh jam tarts when the king had to make do with a warmed-over flan, talked for a few moments with Morgan, then left. The rest of the time Sir Kai, Sir Bedivere, Sir Arnald, Sir Bors, Sir Ywain, Sir Lionel, Gawain's brothers Sir Gaheris and Sir Agrivaine, and a few other knights argued about international affairs. At last the arguments grew improbable and the arguers incomprehensible, and Terence led the most unstable knights back to their own rooms to sleep off their wine.

The next morning the king announced that he would hold a state dinner that evening in honor of King Ban and his court. Terence chose Gawain's court clothes, pressed them with a hot iron, and polished Gawain's black leather boots. Gawain scornfully rejected all the frills and jewels that were popular among the continental knights, but at a state dinner even Gawain had to dress with care.

Shortly before the banquet, Morgan came to Gawain's chambers, where Terence was carefully snipping unruly hairs from Gawain's red beard. She was magnificently dressed in a pale lavender gown, and her long blonde hair was gathered simply behind her head and then allowed to fall freely down her back. Gawain chuckled. "It's amazing what a bit of primping can do to hide the years, isn't it, Terence?"

Morgan was only a year older than Gawain, but he seldom missed a chance to tease her about her age.

Evidently Morgan was in a good mood, because she only smiled good-naturedly and said, "Terence, don't cut too much off. We don't want the court to know that this youngster's beard hasn't come in full yet."

"I wish both of you would leave me out of this," Terence muttered.

"You're in a good mood this evening, Auntie. Plotting mischief?" Gawain asked.

Morgan smiled dreamily and said, "I plan only to be the most beautiful woman at the banquet."

"A delightful plan," Gawain said drily. "Sure to make you many friends among the ladies."

"I do not seek friends among the ladies, Gawain."

Gawain grunted. "Where are you sitting tonight?"

Morgan smiled faintly. "I sit at the king's table this evening. I hope I do not outshine his charming queen."

"Jade," Gawain muttered, but Morgan had left.

Terence glanced at the door. "Why do you like her so much, milord?"

Gawain smiled crookedly. "You must admit that she's never dull."

Terence brushed whiskers from Gawain's chest and shoulders. "She's vain and selfish and spiteful and everything that you would hate in someone else."

"She isn't always selfish," Gawain said.

"Only when she's awake?"

Gawain smiled briefly, but his eyes were serious. "I remember someone she used to care for, a little girl named Elaine. Morgan used to take Elaine riding, make daisy chains with her, tell her stories."

Terence tried to imagine the cold sorceress playing with a little girl and found he could not. "Where is Elaine now?"

"She died when she was thirteen. Scarlet fever. It was the only time I've ever seen Morgan cry. She was more mother and sister to Elaine than aunt."

"She was her aunt?" Terence asked, his eyes widening.

"Elaine was my little sister," Gawain said. "Morgan and I cried together."

"I'm sorry, milord."

"So you see why I put up with Morgan, even at her most provoking," Gawain said with a smile.

She was certainly provoking that night at the banquet, and Queen Guinevere was the one provoked. As soon as Morgan entered the hall in her finery and Guinevere learned that Morgan was to sit at the head table, the queen became visibly enraged. It wasn't that she was jealous of Arthur, Terence reflected, because the king showed Morgan only the same gentle courtesy he used with all the court ladies. It was Morgan's beauty. A beautiful woman herself,

Guinevere was not used to being eclipsed by another.

Guinevere showed her anger obliquely, but it was no less obvious. She greeted Morgan with bright and brittle laughter, covered her with effusive compliments uttered in a voice that was rather too loud, and succeeded only in drawing attention to the two of them. Morgan, accepting the queen's artificial prattle with only an amused smile, looked much more queenly than the queen.

"Why, Lady Morgan," Guinevere said brightly, "I declare that you are so brave! I should never dare to wear a gown of that shade if my hair were your color!"

"Would you not?" Morgan's voice dripped boredom, but when she glanced at Gawain, her eyes glinted with mischief.

"Poor Guinevere," Gawain said softly to Terence. "You know she might have a friend if she would stop competing with everyone."

"Just tell her that she's beautiful," Terence whispered. "You'll be her best friend at once."

"That's not what I meant."

Arthur, meanwhile, talked gravely with King Ban and with Sir Kai, his stepbrother and most trusted advisor, apparently unaware of the minor drama beside him.

Before the evening was over, though, no one was thinking about Guinevere's behavior. As the servants cleared the second course, a frightened page dashed into the banquet hall and whispered urgently to King Arthur. The king questioned the boy sharply, then whispered some terse instructions. More frightened than ever, the page turned on his heel and ran back out of the hall. All conversation stopped as Arthur rose and said, "I beg your pardon for interrupting your meal, but I'm afraid I must attend to some business. Kai, will you come with me, please?"

Arthur and Sir Kai began to follow the page, but before they had gone two steps, the door flew open and a procession of twelve elderly men in white robes filed into the banquet hall. Each man carried an olive branch. The man in front, somewhat younger than the rest and much more belligerent-looking, stopped in front of the head table and said, "I seek one Arthur, who styles himself King of the Britons!"

King Arthur returned to his place and deliberately took his seat. "I am one Arthur," he said mildly.

"We are emissaries of Lucius, Emperor of Rome and all its dominions," the man said.

"You've come all the way from Rome?" Arthur asked. "You must be weary. Please join our little family dinner. We can discuss your business tomorrow."

"We do not eat with rebels," the man pronounced grandly.

"They've never come from Rome," King Ban

interrupted. "And Lucius is no more Emperor of Rome than your horse. He's some sort of minor excise official, Procurator of Gaul or something, who's gotten a big idea of himself. He's a nuisance to all of us in France."

The leader of the delegation flushed darkly, and Arthur said, "Ah, you've just come from France. Then I do not wonder that you decline our dinner. Those channel crossings can be very unsettling. Perhaps you would rather rest for the evening. We can deal with your business tomorrow."

"The Emperor does not choose to wait!" the man declared.

"Very understandable," Arthur said, nodding. "I find myself much in sympathy with him. I, for instance, am waiting for the third course."

Gawain's shoulders shook, and Sir Kai smiled widely. The ambassador frowned and said, "I have a decree from your lord the Emperor, and I will read it to you now, whatsoever say ye."

Arthur sighed and said, "Very well. And when you are done, perhaps you would join us after all. We have roast venison, and my cook really makes a good thing of it."

The man ignored the king and took out a roll of parchment. In a grand voice he read, "The high and mighty Emperor Lucius sendeth to the self-styled

King of Britain greeting, commanding that he acknowledge him for his lord and send him the truage due of this realm unto the Empire, which his father and other tofore his predecessors have paid as is of record—"

"I'm sorry," Arthur interrupted. "But is there much more? I fear the venison will grow cold."

The man shook with anger. "Is this how you treat your visitors of state?" he demanded.

Slowly Arthur rose. "Sirrah, I have given you three opportunities to behave as a visitor of state. I sent word that I would see you in the entrance hall, but you chose to interrupt our dinner instead. I twice suggested that we conduct state business tomorrow, as would be seemly, but you refused. I no longer consider you visitors of state. I consider you and your eleven friends only bothersome intruders to whom little attention and no courtesy are due."

"If you do not send tribute to Lucius, he will burn your land!" the ambassador cried.

"I shall keep it in mind," Arthur said. "Await my summons in the entrance hall. If you interrupt me again, I will have you flogged by my scullery maids." Arthur gestured to three burly knights, who firmly escorted the twelve ambassadors from the banquet hall. Arthur turned immediately to King Ban. "Ban, what can you tell me about this Lucius? Has he an army?"

King Ban nodded. "He arrived with one regiment as an escort. Mostly foot soldiers. But more troops have been arriving. I did not think that he had grown so strong, but he would hardly make such a demand without an army to support him."

"So even if he's acting on his own, he may have some support from the Empire," Arthur looked around him. "What advice do I hear, my knights?"

"Pay them nothing!" a gruff voice called out.

"That would mean war, Pellinore," Arthur said.

The knight who had spoken looked startled. "Yes, my liege. Do you...do you not wish for war?"

"Only a fool wishes for war," Arthur said. "Do I hear any other counsel?" No one spoke. The king waited for a long minute, then nodded. "I too see no other option. Either we pay these cockerels tribute, which I will not do, or we fight. How shall we go about it? Kai?"

Sir Kai turned to King Ban. "How many troops can this Lucius raise, sir? Your highest guess."

"Surely he would not dare to send such a message with less than twenty thousand," King Ban said after a moment.

"We can raise that many, my liege," Sir Kai said, "but it will take months."

"Which will give Lucius time to cross the channel," Arthur answered. "And I'd rather not let him 'burn our lands,' as this gentleman put it. But there is a faster way to raise an army." He turned to King Ban. "You called this Lucius a nuisance, I believe?"

King Ban grinned broadly. "Indeed, sir. If you would not take it amiss, I should be delighted to join you in your endeavor. I shall return to Benouic at once and have my son prepare our troops. We will be ready by the time you arrive."

Arthur bowed grandly and said, "Bring the ambassadors back in."

Still flushed with anger, the spokesman for the delegation was ushered back into the banquet hall. "I am not used to being treated like a lackey," he said.

"Really?" Arthur answered politely. "How fortunate for you. I have a reply for your master, but I'm afraid I haven't had time to have it inscribed yet. Do you think you can remember it?"

The man turned even redder and said, "I shall do my best."

"Tell your master to go to the devil."

The man's eyes looked as if they would pop out. "Your answer is rebellion!" he announced incredulously.

"No," Arthur said firmly. "My answer is war."

⟨ﳐﱞ⟩

Gawain took part in the first skirmish of the war. It began with a diplomatic mission. Arthur had swiftly gathered an army and crossed the channel to the continent to meet King Ban. Now, Arthur and Ban were camped only a mile from Lucius's fortifications. To all appearances, Lucius was outnumbered, and Arthur sent Gawain, Sir Bors, Sir Lionel, and Sir Bedivere to offer Lucius the chance to surrender. Though under the protection of a white flag, Gawain and the others were set on from behind and had to fight desperately to escape back to Arthur's camp. All four made it alive, but all were injured. Battered and bloody, Gawain reported to Arthur briefly— "They do not choose to surrender, my liege"—and then Terence helped him back to their own tent.

Gawain had a vicious-looking gash in his side and a deep cut in his sword arm, among what seemed like a thousand lesser cuts and bruises. Terence washed off the blood, then tightly bound Gawain's arm and side. When he was through, Gawain pushed himself to a sitting position.

"You lie still, milord. You've lost a lot of blood."

"No, I haven't," Gawain said.

"Yes, you have," Terence said. "Look at that!" He gestured at the pile of bloody rags he had thrown behind him.

"It's not all mine," Gawain said.

"Well, it should have been," Terence muttered.

"Whatever possessed you to go fighting the whole army by yourself, I'd like to know."

"No no, not by myself," Gawain protested. "There were four of us, remember."

"Crack-brain," Terence said bluntly.

"They started it—" Gawain began, then broke off suddenly. "Why am I explaining myself to you?"

Terence snorted. "Can you think of someone else who'd bother to listen? I hope you realize you can't fight tomorrow," he added.

Gawain lifted his wounded sword arm and tried a few motions. He winced. "I could fight left-handed," he suggested. Terence looked pointedly at the wound in Gawain's left side, and Gawain shrugged. "How about if I only fight in the morning, and come back to camp after noon?"

This was more reasonable than it sounded. Years before, when he and Terence had first met, Gawain had been granted a special boon by Trevisant, the hermit who had raised Terence: Gawain's strength would rise and decline as the sun rose and fell. But Terence was not convinced. "And what would you do? Stop in the middle of a fight? Tip your hat and say that you're terribly sorry, but you have to be off?"

Gawain grinned. "It would be difficult, wouldn't it? How about if I prepare for battle but only watch? I won't fight unless things start to go bad for Arthur.

Promise." Terence put a stern and dissatisfied expression on his face, but this concession was already more than he had hoped for, and he nodded. "Thank you, Mother," Gawain said.

And so it was that on the following day, when the two full armies met, Gawain and Terence sat on their horses on a hill that overlooked the battlefield. The day began with a cavalry charge. Arthur had divided his forces into two parts, and King Ban's men made a third. At dawn, Arthur's first group charged Lucius's lines from the east. Then, with King Ban's men awaiting their signal, Arthur's second group attacked from the north. At first Lucius's troops fell back, but before long the lines steadied, and the warriors settled down to hard battle.

Then, to Terence's amazement, Arthur's troops began to retreat, step by step. Every Roman warrior who fell was replaced immediately by another, and then by two, and then three. Roman soldiers seemed to be springing from the earth itself, there were so many of them. "Where are they coming from, milord?" Terence asked.

"This Lucius is no fool," Gawain said. "He concealed most of his troops until he saw what he was up against."

A trumpeter gave the signal, and King Ban's men raised a jubilant shout and charged into the battle.

Leading the way was a knight in brilliant silver armor, the sort of armor that any one of the court dandies would have sold his soul to own. Terence sniffed and glanced with pride at his master's dented hauberk. You could always tell which knights were fighters and which were brightly dressed puppets.

"Who is that knight in the lead?" Gawain said, whistling softly.

"The one with the pretty armor, you mean?" Terence asked. "I hope he doesn't get it scuffed."

"He might not, at that," Gawain said. "What a horseman!"

Surprised, Terence looked again at the racing knight, who had just hit the Roman lines and disappeared into the chaos of waving arms and lances. With a rush, the rest of King Ban's men arrived at the battle, and the Romans began falling back again. Soon they were back almost to their tents and surrounding fortifications. The silver knight was everywhere, and where he went, Romans fell and the Britons and French surged forward. Gawain whistled appreciatively.

"I'd like to meet this—" he broke off. "Now who the devil is that?"

Terence followed his eyes and saw a regiment of knights making their way through a dense stand of trees at the foot of the hill where he and Gawain sat.

One knight raised a standard, and Terence made out the golden eagle of the Roman legions. It was another troop of Romans, preparing to charge the British and French soldiers from behind.

Gawain put on his helm. "You stay here, Terence."

"Not likely," Terence said shortly, stringing his longbow.

Gawain hesitated only a second, then said, "Right. Shout as loudly as you can on the way down. Now!" He booted his great horse, Guingalet, and tore off down the hill, yelling like a banshee.

Occupied with guiding his horse down the hill, Terence heard, rather than saw, Gawain meet the Romans: there was a crash, followed by a scream of pain, followed by more crashes. He looked up and saw Gawain holding his great sword Galatine in his left hand, doggedly defending himself against three knights. Terence slipped from his horse, clutching his longbow and arrows, and began shooting into the melee. He was able to draw some of the Romans away from Gawain, but they immediately charged at Terence.

They never got to him. A strange knight in black armor galloped past Terence into the battle. With a careless backhand blow, the black knight unhorsed one of those charging Terence and then went to Gawain's aid. In a few seconds, the new knight had freed Gawain from his opponents, and then together they charged into the Roman line. A shrill cry from his left drew Terence's attention, and there, galloping full-tilt across the battlefield, came the silver knight who had led King Ban's charge.

It was a glorious battle, and over in a minute. The black knight, the silver knight, and Gawain fought brilliantly and furiously. The Roman regiment, thrown into disarray, recoiled, tried to regroup, then recoiled again. Then, suddenly, the remaining Roman knights threw up their hands in surrender. The sounds of battle ceased. Terence looked across the field and saw that the other Romans had surrendered as well.

Gawain turned to the black knight and said, "Sir knight, I am doubly in your debt. You saved my squire's life as well as my own."

"And you, in your turn, saved my battle," the knight said, raising his visor. It was King Arthur. "I thank you."

"My liege!" Gawain exclaimed.

Arthur turned back toward the captive knights. "I am Arthur, King of the Britons and master of all England. Where is this Lucius, who calls himself Emperor of Rome?" A knight pointed wordlessly at one of the bodies stretched out nearby. "That one?" Arthur asked. The knight nodded, and Arthur said, "So that is why all the others have surrendered?"

The knight said, "No one to pay us now."

"I see," Arthur said. "You are not Romans at all, are you?"

"We are whatever pleases the one who pays us," the knight replied. "Now we are nothing."

"See that in the future you remain nothing before you fight against England or Benouic," Arthur said. "Go."

The mercenary knight hesitated for a second, then wheeled his horse and galloped away, leading the rest of Lucius's hired troops. In a few minutes, the battlefield held only the Britons, the French, and the dead. The silver knight who had fought beside Gawain and Arthur dismounted, walked to Arthur's side, and knelt.

"My father has told me of your wisdom," he said emotionally, in heavily accented English, "but now it is that I have myself seen your valor and your graciousness. To so great a king, I offer myself as his servant for the rest of my life."

"I have enough servants," Arthur said gently. "But I would be proud to call such a warrior my knight. Who is your father?"

"King Ban of Benouic, your highness."

"You are Ban's son?" Arthur looked startled.

"Yes, your highness. I am called Sir Lancelot."

II

THE GREEN KNIGHT

Sir Lancelot, the hero of Arthur's victory, remained in France after the battle, but he declared his intention of soon following the English army to Camelot and becoming a knight of the Round Table. All the English were pleased and sang Sir Lancelot's praises almost without ceasing. Indeed, by the time they had arrived home, Terence was thoroughly sick of hearing Sir Lancelot toasted as the Flower of All Chivalry and the Greatest Knight of All Time. Knights and ladies who had always toasted Gawain as the greatest of all Arthur's knights could now talk of nothing but the imminent arrival of Sir Lancelot.

The king planned a victory ball, but delayed it so that Sir Lancelot could be present. But Sir Lancelot did not come. After waiting two weeks, Arthur shrugged and held the ball without him. Terence and

Gawain went to the dance, of course, but neither of them looked forward to the evening, Gawain because his wounds still pained him and Terence because he was weary of hearing people speculate on the wonderful Sir Lancelot's whereabouts.

So it happened that as the dancing began, Terence and Gawain stood apart from the crowd. After a few minutes, the king strolled over and joined them. "How are your wounds healing?" Arthur asked Gawain.

Gawain answered frankly. "Slowly. Or perhaps I am only impatient."

"Or perhaps you fought too hard after being hurt. I do not forget that you were weak and wounded when you charged that regiment, Gawain."

"I wish you would, my king. I ask no thanks."

The king nodded gravely and turned the subject. "Perhaps Morgan could do something for you."

"No doubt she could, if she were here," Gawain answered. "And if she felt like it."

"Ah, she is gone, then," Arthur said, nodding. "Perhaps it is as well. I believe that her presence sometimes upsets the ladies." Arthur moved away, and Terence unconsciously looked around for Queen Guinevere. Unquestionably the most beautiful woman at court now that Morgan was absent, the queen was in high good spirits, dancing with Sir Bagdemagus.

Just then, there was a stir at the great doors of the ballroom. Terence glanced over, then stared. There, amid a bevy of admiring ladies, was the long-awaited Sir Lancelot. He wore brilliant continental clothing, a vision in expensive fabric, from satin shoes with long curling toes to a muffin-shaped green silk hat. Eagerly, Sir Lancelot crossed the floor to Arthur. "My seigneur!" he cried. "I am desolate that I have taken so long to arrive, and now to interrupt this grand *fête!* It is too bad! And here am I in my traveling clothes!"

The king's eyes widened, but he bowed in gracious greeting. "You are welcome at any time, Sir Lancelot," he said. "Er...those are your traveling clothes?"

"But yes!" Sir Lancelot replied. "I must go at once to change to my good clothes, no?"

"Perhaps you could be persuaded to join us as you are," Arthur said gently. "The ball is partly in your honor, after all."

The ladies eagerly added their appeals, and Sir Lancelot allowed himself to be persuaded. Terence, watching them from his squirely place a few steps behind his master, snorted, a bit louder than he had intended. Gawain glanced at him, one eyebrow raised, then stepped back beside him.

"Jealous, Terence?" he asked.

"Aren't you?" Terence replied bluntly.

"Mortifying as it is, I'm afraid I am. I used to scorn the admiration of the crowds. Now that they've forgotten me, it's harder."

"You fought in that battle, too," Terence muttered. "Why does everyone look only at Sir Lancelot?"

"Maybe because he's better looking," Gawain said with a smile.

It was true. Lancelot was impossibly good looking. His face was smooth and firm without having the hint of wild cragginess that marked Gawain's. His eyes were a brilliant blue. His shoulders were broad and manly, his hips lean, and his legs muscular and well-shaped. Terence nodded and said, "Pretty clothes, too."

Gawain's lips twitched slightly. "Well, they're not in my style, I think."

Gawain joined Sir Kai near a plate of ham, and they talked until the dance ended. Across the room Terence saw the king talking to the queen. In a minute the king crossed to where Gawain and Sir Kai stood. Guinevere and her ladies-in-waiting followed.

"Kai," he said when he was near enough to be heard, "how are our horses after the battle and crossing. In good shape?"

Sir Kai nodded.

Guinevere smiled delightedly. "There!" she said. "I knew there was no reason we couldn't!"

Arthur sighed. "Well enough to stand a tournament, do you think?"

"A tournament?" Sir Kai asked blankly.

"The ladies would like us to hold a tournament to honor Sir Lancelot's acceptance as a knight of the Round Table," Arthur said quietly. "Can we do it?"

Sir Kai glared balefully at Guinevere and said, "It would be very difficult now, my king."

Arthur shook his head. "The truth, Kai. Can we do it?"

Sir Kai scowled. "Yes, sire."

Arthur turned to Guinevere. "Very well, my love. We shall hold a tournament."

Several of the ladies squealed with delight and clapped ecstatically. One of them called out loudly, "Oh Sir Lancelot, did you hear? The king is holding a tournament for you!"

Sir Lancelot walked over to the group. "Do you so, your highness?"

"I do, Sir Lancelot."

"You honor me beyond my deserts, your highness." Sir Lancelot bowed.

Arthur said, "I only hope that you do not put us all to shame."

"But no!" Sir Lancelot said. "Truly, I expect to find much difficulty."

Arthur looked over the crowd of ladies behind Guinevere and said, "You may find your greatest difficulty will be in choosing which lady's favor you will wear to the tournament."

The ladies giggled, but most of them turned inviting eyes to Sir Lancelot. Sir Lancelot looked at them, and then his eyes met the queen's. He gazed at her, enraptured, then knelt before her. "After seeing such beauty as yours, fair lady, how could I ask a favor from another? If you will allow me to compete for your honor in this tournament, then tell me so by telling me your name."

The queen blushed even more fiercely and in a faint voice said, "My name is Guinevere, Sir Lancelot."

Sir Lancelot looked stricken. "Guinevere? But that . . . you are . . ."

The king's face showed nothing. "It was not so difficult, after all," he said. "Sir Lancelot, I am honored that you should bear my queen's standard."

Both Sir Lancelot and Guinevere looked at Arthur. Sir Lancelot's face showed shock and despair, Guinevere's a pathetic and strangely sorrowful defiance.

◈

The tournament concluded as everyone had expected and most had hoped: Sir Lancelot won the day, apparently without exerting himself. When he knelt before the queen and offered her the prize—a dainty grey mare—his shining armor was barely scratched, and he was not even breathing heavily. Guinevere's eyes sparkled as she accepted Sir Lancelot's tribute. Gawain, whose wounds had kept him from competing and who had watched the tournament from the king's pavilion, leaned close to Arthur and said, "It is gracefully given, my king."

"And rapturously received," Arthur said drily. Gawain was silent, and in a moment Arthur said, "For my love, Gawain, will you forget that I said that?"

"For your love, my liege, it is already forgotten."

Arthur stood and congratulated the victor, thanked all the participants, and declared the games concluded. The crowd cheered lustily for Sir Lancelot, and the queen beamed as if they were applauding her instead of the knight at her feet.

Within two weeks, all that the court could talk of was the queen and Sir Lancelot. Sir Lancelot's eyes were seldom away from Guinevere, and his gaze spoke clearly of abject worship. As for Guinevere, she was in the brightest of moods, laughing and enjoying the hero's adoration. Many considered this situation appalling and nearly wept to see the king's gentle kindness to his lady received so. Others though — particularly the continental knights and courtiers — seemed to find the whole affair exceedingly romantic. For some reason, Sir Lancelot's love for Guinevere was thought more true than Arthur's. Terence even heard a French minstrel sing that true Courtly Love must always be for the wife of another. To Terence, raised by a holy man in a hermitage, such a theory was astounding, but to the French courtiers it seemed only logical.

In the end, this difference of opinion divided Camelot. Two distinct camps arose: one that honored the French ideal of Courtly Love — with Guinevere and Sir Lancelot as its embodiment — and another that honored loyalty to Arthur and condemned the affair. The first group, by far the larger, collected around Sir Lancelot, and the second coalesced around Sir Kai and Gawain. This second group gathered in Gawain's chambers, an extension of his late-night drinking sessions.

Only the king refused to identify himself with either group, and only in his unifying presence could both groups meet without discord. Terence found his respect for the king growing every day. Surrounded by those who openly celebrated his betrayal by his wife, still he ruled all with justice and compassion. His humanity may have been wounded, but his kingliness remained untouched.

Only a very few saw how deeply he was hurt. One misty dawn on the wall of the castle, Gawain and Terence caught one of these rare glimpses. Word had come to Camelot that Sir Tor was finally returning from his long quest, and they had gone up to the wall to look for him. There they found Arthur quietly gazing across the fields. In the grey distance, two figures on horseback met by the edge of the woods. No one could mistake Lancelot's white charger and Guinevere's grey mare. Arthur watched them until they disappeared in the woods, then wearily looked up.

"Hello, nephew. Terence."

Gawain nodded. "My liege."

Arthur took a deep breath. "I'm glad to see you, Gawain. For some time I've wished to speak with you."

"I am at your service, sire. Terence, wait for me below."

Arthur smiled. "Quite unnecessary. I feel sure that Terence knows more than either of us about the goings on of the court. And I know I can trust him." Gawain nodded, and Arthur continued. "I've always had the impression, Gawain, that you understand better than others the heart of a maiden."

"No, sire. But I know something of the pain of love." Gawain's eyes clouded, as they always did

32

when he thought of Lorie, the faery princess whom he loved across the worlds.

"Does Guinevere love him?"

Gawain hesitated, then spoke gently. "Forgive me, sire, but I do not think the queen is able to love anyone very deeply."

"Anyone?"

"No, sire. For her, love is the trappings of love — love letters, whispered compliments, gifts. It is like Sir Griflet's notion of knighthood — strong on armor and banners and riding peacocky horses in tournament parades, but short on honor and sacrifice. I do not think that Guinevere has ever known love as you have known it."

Arthur looked absently at the forest. "And I am not easy to love, am I?"

"No. You are the king, the master of all you behold, the servant of none."

"And Lancelot?"

"He is her slave."

Slowly, a tear formed in Arthur's eye, then rolled down his cheek. Terence, ashamed to look on his king's grief, turned away. His own eyes misted. Gawain's eyes, too, were bright with tears. "Am I a fool to love her, Gawain?"

"If so, it is a divine foolishness," Gawain said. Gawain's tears flowed more freely, and he gazed into the morning mist as if looking into the Other World. The King of all Britain and the Maiden's Knight mingled their misery in the growing day.

That afternoon Tor and Plogrun returned to Camelot, and with them, on a silky white palfrey, rode Morgan Le Fay. As was usual when a knight returned from a quest, the king called for a meeting of the Round Table to hear Tor recount his adventures. His tale was full, and Tor made the most of it. He had traveled the length of the island and defeated many wandering knights; he had fought the fierce Redshank Danes, seafaring marauders from the east and, as he put it, had seen "many sights near too wondrous to believe and far too wondrous to recount." Even the French minstrels admitted that Tor had told his tale well.

After the official telling, though, Tor and Plogrun went with Gawain, Terence, and Morgan to Gawain's chambers for a private reunion. Tor told of packs of hounds with human faces—"The Conn Annown," Morgan said, nodding—and a ghostly wooden banquet hall decorated with the grisly limbs of defeated enemies, where each night food and strong drink appeared and each morning disappeared again, eaten by no one knows whom. Morgan listened with interest and said, "I had heard of this hall, but had hardly believed it real." It was clear to Terence that Tor's quest had taken him, if not actually into the Other World, at least to its threshold, and he was glad that his friends had tasted the wonders of that realm.

After a while, Tor broke off his account suddenly and said, "Say Gawain, I don't know if you've heard: old Marhault's dead." Years before, Gawain and Tor had set out on a quest together and had been joined there by a great Cornish knight named Sir Marhault.

Gawain shook his head. "How did it happen?"

"I'm not sure. We just found his marker in Cornwall one day. It said he was killed by one Sir Tristram."

"I've heard of Tristram," Gawain said reflectively. "But Marhault was one of the best. I didn't think the knight lived who could do it."

"There's always a better knight, Gawain," Morgan said. Terence couldn't tell if she meant to warn her nephew or to mock him.

"Speaking of better knights, who's this popinjay Lancelot I hear about," Tor asked.

"Don't you know?" Gawain replied. "He's the greatest knight in England."

"Ay, that's what I hear. That's what they say in Cornwall about Tristram, too. And it's what I've always said about you, Gawain. You can't all be the greatest knight in England."

"Why not?" Gawain smiled suddenly. "It makes for better stories that way."

Tor grunted. "Well, is this latest greatest knight as good as they say?"

"He is. That's the galling part of it. He's a wizard with a lance."

Tor hesitated, then said, "And is the rest of it true?"

"The rest of what?"

"Guinevere."

"It's true," Gawain said.

Morgan leaned forward with sudden interest, "And Arthur?"

"Unhappy. Can you doubt it?"

She shook her head. "He deserves a better lady than Guinevere. If only—" She broke off.

"If only?" Gawain asked.

She smiled ruefully. "Like Lancelot, I find that the forbidden love is the sweetest."

"Poor Morgan," Gawain said simply.

"But where Lancelot's love is forbidden by custom, mine is forbidden by blood," she said. "And even an enchantress is bound by blood." Gawain nodded.

Tor smiled, but without rancor. "So, the beautiful woman who has captivated so many men, finds herself a captive to love."

Morgan glanced at him briefly, without comment.

"Is there some way to help my Arthur?" she asked, and no one answered.

By Christmas, still none of them had found an answer. Morgan left the court, and Terence envied her escape. Sir Lancelot and Queen Guinevere grew more obvious every day, and the king showed his misery in the weary lines at his eyes. In his throne room, he was solemn and correct, seldom showing the quiet humor that had distinguished his court before. At the meetings of the Round Table, he was silent and morose. He began to leave the court every now and then to meditate and pray alone at a nearby abbey, often for a week or more. Remembering the peace of the hermitage where he was raised, Terence thought he understood the king's retreats, but Gawain did not. Gawain had known few priests or monks whom he could honor, and he saw Arthur's need for religious exercise as a sign of weakness. In any case, Arthur always seemed invigorated when he returned.

The preparations for the annual Christmas feast began, but seldom had Terence felt less festive. Sir Lancelot and Guinevere spent hours together, planning their wardrobes for the feast, which always lasted from Christmas Eve until the New Year. On the first night, Gawain sat at the king's table, with Guinevere, Sir Kai, and Sir Lancelot. To everyone except Sir Lancelot, gazing enraptured at the queen, and Guinevere, basking in his attentions, the feast was oppressively slow. Even the king commented on the dullness of the banquet, saying that he almost wished that the Emperor of Rome would send another delegation with a challenge.

By way of entertainment, a bard told a heroic tale about the ancient hero Cucholinn, which lightened the air somewhat, but this bard was followed immediately by a French minstrel who sang a long ballad about Sir Tristram of Cornwall and his love affair with Queen Isoult, the wife of King Mark of Cornwall. The king listened politely, but grimly, and at the end of the evening all the company wished they did not have to return the following night. They did, though, and each night's banquet seemed longer than the last. Terence suggested that they go off questing before the next long feast, and Gawain heartily assented.

Excitement finally arrived on the seventh night. As the fourth course was being cleared, a muffled exclamation came from the kitchen, followed by an eerie silence. A moment later the wide kitchen doors flew open so violently that they splintered against the wall. Then, through the gaping doorway rode the largest man that Terence had ever seen, mounted on the largest horse, and from the top of the man's head to the horse's hooves, they were both as green as the grass in June. He wore no armor and was bareheaded, but no one could doubt that this giant was a knight, for his fierce, bearded face was noble, and in his right hand he held a wicked-looking axe. The green knight stopped in the center of the room, gazed around him, then spoke in a rumbling voice, "Where is the chief of this crowd? Long have I wished to see so famed a sire."

Arthur stood and said, "I bid you fair welcome, good knight. I am the chief of this assembly — Arthur, by name. Come join our celebration, I pray you, and on the morrow we shall hear your purpose."

The knight examined Arthur's face, then nodded, as if to himself. "Nay, I thank you, O king, but the high lord who sent me did not intend me to tarry. My errand is to test this high court, whose praises are so puffed off, called so peerless in passage of arms and in courage so complete."

"If it is a fight that you wish, you shall surely not go away unrequited," Arthur said, "though I should have to fight you myself."

Gawain started to stand, but the knight said, "I come to seek no combat, O king. I see none at this board but beardless children, pitiful and puny before me. I offer but a New Year's game for their amusement."

Arthur frowned at the insult to his knights, but he said only, "What manner of game, O knight?"

"Stroke for stroke!" The green knight looked around the room for a third time. "With this axe! I shall bide the first blow, and then exactly one year from today, the knight who chooses to play my New Year's game shall take a blow from me. Who shall play?"

"He's daft," Gawain said amid the resulting hub-bub. "And anyone who'd play a game like this with a faery knight is even more daft."

Arthur nodded in agreement, and opened his mouth to speak, but the green knight spoke first. "What, is this truly Arthur's house? Whose fame is spread so far? Where are all those doughty knights of whom I have heard? Are these they, these who cower and quake before any cut is given?"

Arthur's eyes flashed, and Sir Lancelot spoke up eagerly. "Your highness, let me challenge this ruffi-an to single combat!"

Guinevere started from her seat and exclaimed impulsively, "Lance! No! I couldn't—" She trailed off and looked at the king, wide-eyed.

The lines in Arthur's forehead deepened, and for a second he looked at his queen without expression. Then, in a low voice, he said, "I accept your challenge, O knight. Give me the axe."

The green knight dismounted and all in the hall saw how huge he really was, at least a head taller than any knight present. As Arthur stepped around the table, the knight gave him the axe and knelt before him, ready to take his blow. Arthur lifted the giant axe above his head. No one moved: the green knight waited in unflinching patience, and the rest of the assembly stared transfixed. The queen gazed at Arthur with horrified incomprehension. Then, just as Arthur raised the axe to its highest point, Gawain spoke. "My liege, I beg you, before all these present, to let this knight's challenge be mine."

Terence's throat tightened. Arthur paused, then lowered the axe to the floor. "No, nephew," he said.

"My king, I ask you to be ruled by this company. I honor your wish to face your court's trial yourself, but you must not. You are the heart of this land."

Arthur looked weary beyond words. "And you," he said, "are the greatest of all my knights."

"My only honor, O king, is that I serve you. Give me the axe." Gawain turned to the rest of the assembly and said, "Which of us shall it be?"

One by one the knights of the Round Table indicated Gawain. Tor's face twisted with grief, and Sir Kai's deep eyes looked empty, but both of them pointed at Gawain.

King Arthur heard his court's judgment and without a word laid the axe at his feet and returned to his seat. Gawain looked quickly at Terence and whispered, "I'm sorry, lad." Terence felt suddenly,

41

unreasonably calm. He nodded, and Gawain walked to the axe.

Through all of these proceedings, the green knight had waited patiently. Now he spoke. "Before going further, tell me your name, O knight."

"I am called Gawain."

The knight's eyes lit with unmistakable satisfaction. "Sir Gawain! By Gog, I am wondrous pleased it should be you! And in one year's time, you will come to me for the answering blow?"

"I will. Wherever you say."

"I am the Knight of the Green Chapel, and I am known by many. You shall have no difficulty finding me." With that, the faery knight bowed his head and bared the nape of his neck. Gawain looked at it grimly, then raised the axe and struck with all his power. The knight's head flipped cleanly from his shoulders, and his body sprawled limply on the floor. Bright red blood poured from the severed neck, startling in its contrast to the green head and body. Ladies moaned weakly, and more than half of them fainted or pretended to. Among the knights there was an audible sigh of relief, but the sigh broke off abruptly. Slowly the green knight's arms began to move. They braced themselves and pushed the headless trunk from the floor. On hands and knees, the knight's body groped for a second until it found its head. Then, holding the still dripping member, the body stood. While all the court stared in horror, the green eyelids flickered open and blinked as the eyes beneath focused on Gawain.

"Do not forget, Sir Gawain. One year from today at the Green Chapel. You have this day richly deserved that your neck should have my blow next New Year's Eve."

And with that, the Knight of the Green Chapel vaulted easily onto his giant horse and galloped away, leaving a trail of flinty sparks where his horse's hooves struck the hard and bloody floor.

III

SETTING OFF

Gawain's next three months at Camelot were wretched for everyone. The moment that the Green Knight disappeared, Gawain became the center of the court's attention. It seemed to occur suddenly and simultaneously to all the court that Gawain had done something surpassingly courageous, and knights who for months had given all praise to Sir Lancelot realized that when it had been a question of the king's life or his own, it had been Gawain who had acted. All treated Gawain with hushed and awed respect, quietly stepping aside to make way for him wherever he walked—"As if I were a blamed ghost," Gawain commented to Tor, chuckling.

Terence did not enjoy the court's renewed respect for his master, since it arose primarily from Gawain's imminent death. No one at Camelot doubted that Gawain had but a year to live. Only an elf-man or a wizard could have survived decapitation, as the Green Knight had, and Gawain was neither. Gawain's comment about being treated as if he were a ghost was more correct than he intended: in the eyes of many, he was the next thing to a ghost already.

Gawain himself, perhaps as a perverse response to the court's morbid awe, was cheerful, almost jovial. Much against his inclination, Terence vowed to follow Gawain's example, at least in public. Arthur, too, seemed to be in better spirits than before. No longer did the king openly brood over Guinevere and Sir Lancelot. He dealt with affairs of state with something like his former zest, and he spent much time with Sir Kai, Gawain, Sir Bedivere, and other particular friends and advisors. Terence did not know what it was, but something had happened to Arthur at that feast to renew him.

One dark morning, on his way to the stables, Terence saw a solitary figure on the castle wall. Recognizing the king, Terence returned to his chambers and told Gawain. Gawain's forehead creased, and he said, "Let's go see."

It was indeed the king, at the same post where they had seen him before, looking out into the blackness. He heard them coming and looked up. "Hello, Gawain. Good morning, Terence."

"Good morning, my king," Gawain said. Terence bowed.

"Come to check on me?" Gawain nodded. "I'm all right," Arthur said.

"Are they out there again?" Gawain asked.

Arthur looked into the dark, then shook his head. "I don't know. I was just wondering myself." Terence was close enough now to see the king's face, and in it was none of the barely submerged pain that had been there the last time they had met on this wall. The king shrugged and said, "It will always matter to me whether my wife loves me, but her love is not the only love in the world." The king smiled. "My nephew, it seems, loves me enough to die for me."

"Your nephew is not alone in that willingness, sire."

The king nodded. "I know—Kai, Bedivere, Tor, Ywain, all of you. I am ashamed that, surrounded by such friends, I still made such a cake of myself over Guinevere." The king paused and added, "I only wish I could have learned my oversight less dearly." Arthur put his hand on Gawain's shoulder. "Do you think you will return from this Green Chapel?"

"It would be too much to hope, sire."

"It is never too much to hope. I will enjoy your love while you are here, and when you leave I will await your return."

46

As it turned out, Gawain left earlier than anyone had expected. The court's reverence for him continued to grow until Gawain's stature reached almost mythical proportions. People spoke of him in the past tense, as if he were a hero of the misty and mystical past, like the ancient Cucholinn or the Welsh hero Gwalchmai, and told wild and improbable and utterly fanciful tales about Gawain's supposed deeds. Still worse, some began to blame Arthur for Gawain's fate. At first in hushed tones in corners, then increasingly in the open, people began to accuse Arthur of sending his best knight to certain death. Some even suggested that Gawain had trifled with Guinevere, and that this was Arthur's revenge. Finally, one late night in his chambers with Sir Kai and Tor, Gawain decided he had to leave.

"If it's like this after three months," Gawain said, "what will it be like after six?"

"It will get worse," Sir Kai admitted, "but will leaving make things better?"

"I'm sure of it. The court already thinks of me as dead. As soon as I'm not around to remind them of my presence, they'll forget me."

Tor nodded and said grudgingly, "I think you're right. When you're out of sight, the gossips will find something else to chew on. But I hate the thought of your leaving."

"If it's not now, it'll be soon enough. You know that. Maybe once I'm out of sight, you can all get on with living. As it is, I feel I'm attending my own wake."

Tor shook his head doubtfully, but only said, "Well, I'm going with you."

"No."

"Gawain—"

"What could you do? I'm honor bound to let him take his blow at me. You wouldn't stop him, would you?" Tor shook his head. "Let me go alone," Gawain said. "Except...except for..." He turned back to where Terence stood in the shadows. "Lad, I'll understand if you don't wish it, but if you'd come with me, I'd be grateful."

Terence looked at his master with scorn and disbelief in his face. "Are you off your head? You just try to stop me from coming!"

Tor's lips twitched, and he said unsteadily, "How ...how touching." Gawain chuckled, and then they all laughed—perhaps louder and longer than was warranted, but it was good to laugh.

The king argued strenuously when Gawain told him his plans, but for the most part the court treated the announcement with relief. Three months of grieving had been hard on everyone. In the end, even the king had to admit that Gawain's reasons were good, and he gave Gawain his blessing to begin his search for the Green Chapel. Gawain even convinced the king not to hold a farewell banquet by saying he had no wish to attend his own funeral meal, so the only ceremonial recognition of Gawain's departure was the meeting of the Round Table the night before he left.

At this meeting, the knights took turns praising Gawain's courage and unequaled brilliance with weapons and renowned courtesy and so on. One of the French knights read a sonnet he had written about Gawain's right arm. For the most part, the evening was pretty maudlin, but Terence felt his sense of humor rising unbidden, and several times he had to restrain the impulse to smile. The high point of the meeting came when Sir Lancelot rose to give his tribute to the departing champion.

"*Mes chers amis,*" he said, "we have gathered ourselves to give glory to one who has not need of our glories. There is no advice, no help, which we can give him as knights, for he knows all the secrets of knighthood already. He goes now to fight a battle that is of a great difference, a battle against the forces of evil. And so I bring you, Sir Gawain, one whose help you can perhaps use: my own chaplain, Father La Roche."

From the shadows behind Sir Lancelot stepped a

thin, mousy-looking priest whom Terence vaguely remembered seeing in Sir Lancelot's train. It was popular among the continental knights to have a personal chaplain. Some even took them along on quests, perhaps, as Sir Kai said derisively, to administer Last Rites to their masters. Even more than Gawain, Sir Kai held a dim view of priests. The priest held something large and round, like a huge plate, at his side.

"Sir Gawain," he began in a sonorous voice, "as you go forth to fight the demons of the elvish world, the principalities and powers of which the Blessed Apostle spoke, whose end is yet not come though they cannot, again as the Blessed Apostle would say, separate us from the love of Our Lord, as also cannot life nor death nor else too sundry to mention here..." He trailed off and looked helplessly around him, as if somehow to discover in the room what he had been about to say.

"As Sir Gawain goes out," prompted Sir Lancelot.

"As I say, as you go out against divers demonish powers, you shall doubtless find your sword of no avail and your right arm of small puissance. Neither shall your massy mail of chains protect you from the forces of evil, nor indeed your great cuisses and greaves." The priest paused for breath. "Indeed, nor shall your mighty helm or shield, be it of wood or iron, stave off the breath of the flames of hellish device..."

"May as well leave the blame stuff here, you mean?" Gawain asked sweetly. Sir Kai choked, and Father La Roche looked flustered and turned to Sir Lancelot for reassurance.

"Give him the gift, Father," Sir Lancelot said.

The priest collected his thoughts and continued, "And yet, we have indeed protection from these divers dire effects—in the prayers of the Blessed Virgin for our sake, that we may be mighty in her battles, doughty in her cause, single-minded in her defense, holy in her righteousness, rejoicing in her presence, early in her service, frequent in her adoration..." Father La Roche licked his lips and frowned.

"The gift, Father," Sir Lancelot said.

"The gift! And so, brave Sir Gawain, as the Blessed Virgin protects us, so this gift will protect you!" He produced the large plate for all to see.

"It's a shield," Sir Lancelot said.

"It's very nice," Sir Gawain said politely. "I thank you both."

"But wait!" the priest said importantly. "This shield is itself of little use to you. Nor your helm nor your shield, whether of wood or of iron, shall protect you from the divers dire effects... nor, indeed, your massy mail of...of chains...." He turned to Sir Lancelot. "I've said this, haven't I?"

"Most excellently well, Father," Sir Lancelot said encouragingly.

"Then have I finished?"

"The device on the shield, Father."

"Oh yes! Oh, I remember. This shield cannot itself protect you, but behold the device emblazoned on its face!"

Everyone leaned forward to see. On the front of the shield was a simple five-pointed star, made up of five connected lines without a break.

"It's very pretty," Gawain said. "Again, I thank you."

"Tell him about the pentangle, Father," Sir Lancelot said. He looked at Sir Gawain and explained, "It's called a pentangle."

"Oh," Gawain said.

"It is a sign devised by Solomon of old," the priest began. "Because never are the lines broken, it is indeed an endless knot." He paused.

"Yes, I see that. Very clever," Gawain said.

"Well may you wear it on your worthy arms, Sir Gawain. For ever faithful in five-fold fashion have you been. First, in your five senses you are ever faultless. Second, never have your five fingers failed you."

"You're too kind," Gawain murmured.

"Third, all your faith, all your dependence has ever been on the five wounds which Our Lord received on the cross."

"The what?"

Broken out of his rhythm, the priest looked flustered again. "The five wounds — both hands, both feet, and the side. You remember. You have always placed your full dependence on them."

"I see," Gawain said. Sir Kai guffawed loudly, and Gawain nodded. "Please continue, Father."

"Fourth, whenever you battle, your mind is always stayed on the five joys which Mary the Blessed Queen of Heaven had in her child." He paused, either waiting for applause or else just for the inevitable interruption.

Gawain blinked and said, "Terribly religious, aren't I?"

"And the fifth of the five fives which form your life are your five virtues: first your boundless generosity, second your brotherly love, third your pure mind, fourth your pure manners, and fifth your compassion. These five fives are always signified in your peerless pentangle."

"It's...it's very nice. Thank you," Gawain said again.

"Show him the inside, Father," Sir Lancelot said.

"Ah, Sir Gawain, great will be your joy when you see the final attribute of this heavenly shield," the priest said triumphantly. "As all your dependence is ever on the aid of the Blessed Virgin, you shall behold her before you always as you go." With that, the priest reversed the shield and displayed the inside. There, delicately painted in the best French style was a picture of a woman, shown from the waist up. By the halo about her head, Terence guessed that this was supposed to be the Virgin Mary, but few women could have looked less virginal. Her loose robe gapped widely open at the breast, displaying everything that one would expect to find there. Her slight smile was positively seductive.

"The Virgin?" Gawain asked.

"And this shield I present to you, noblest of knights," Father La Roche concluded with a flourish.

Gawain took it and looked at the picture for a long moment, then reverently handed it back to Terence. "Why don't you take this to our rooms, lad?" he whispered. "And take care of it."

"I might just blot out some bits of this picture, though," Terence muttered.

"What, this holy picture? Why, lad?" Gawain was all wide-eyed innocence.

"To preserve that pure mind of yours, of course," Terence retorted as he carried the shield away.

By the time Gawain joined him in their chambers after the meeting, Terence had their gear all packed. Gawain's armor was laid out, and everything else was neatly packed into leather bags. Gawain glanced at the bags with a slight smile and said, "It's time we were setting out again anyway. We've been at court too long."

Terence nodded and said, "Said your goodbyes?"

"Ay."

"All right?"

"Hard to leave Arthur like this," Gawain said. "He says that after I leave, he'll go off to that monastery of his for a while to mumble or do whatever he does there, but other than that, he seems pretty cheerful. Better than he's been for a while."

"Think any of them will get up to see you off, milord?"

"They said they wouldn't, but I expect some will."

"And then you'll have to say goodbye all over again."

Gawain nodded thoughtfully and looked at Terence. For a minute they sat together in silence, then Gawain said, "You sleepy, lad?"

Terence grinned. "Let's go."

An hour later they rode unobserved out of the gates of Camelot. They had never left on a quest in the middle of the night before, but this was a different sort of quest.

IV

QUESTING

Gawain and Terence rode northwest into the heavily forested Welsh hills. Of all Britain, Gawain said, this was the wildest and most dangerous region, so it seemed a likely place to seek the uncanny knight. But, despite the Green Knight's assurance that Gawain would have no difficulty, no one whom they met had heard of either the knight or the Green Chapel.

As they traveled, Terence several times noticed Gawain looking reflectively at his squire. Finally, about a fortnight into their journey, Gawain said, "Terence?"

"Yes, milord?"

"You know that I may not...ah...be returning to Camelot after this quest."

"Being dead, you mean," Terence said.

"Well, yes. And the thing I'm wondering is...if it does happen that way, what will you do?"

"I might be dead, too," Terence pointed out.

Gawain frowned. "True. That's true. But what I mean is, what will you do if I'm dead and you're still alive."

Terence pondered this briefly, then admitted, "I don't know."

"Well, that's what I've been thinking. You need a plan."

"I could go back home to the hermit," Terence suggested.

Gawain shook his head. "No, I've thought of that, but it won't do."

"Why not? I had a good childhood with Trevisant," Terence protested.

"Yes, but that's not your life anymore. You've spent too many years in the world of knights. You should go back to Camelot."

"I won't be someone else's squire," Terence said flatly.

"I mean you should become a knight, stupid!"

"Oh!" Terence sighed. "Why didn't you say so to start with?"

Gawain ignored him. "I've given it a lot of thought, Terence. You're more fit to be a knight than most of the clodpoles at the Round Table. All you need to become a first-rate knight is a bit of instruction."

"And you want to instruct me, eh?" Terence sounded dubious.

Gawain blinked. "You could do worse, you know. I mean, I'm not so bad."

Terence grunted noncommittally. "Instruct me in what?"

"Well, swordsmanship for starters. A knight always starts on the ground. Then the lance. You're already a fair horseman, but riding with a lance is a whole different matter." Gawain grew more intent on his projected lessons. "We'll have to learn something of the battle-axe and mace, though I hope you won't ever have to use them. I suppose we'll pass over the knightly graces and courtesy until last, but that's part of knighthood, too. I think that will be enough for starters."

"Sounds delightful," Terence muttered.

"I promise you it won't take you long," Gawain said reassuringly. "You'll be a natural. Just wait until we start sparring with swords. You'll see."

"Did you bring a spare sword?" This was not really a question, since Terence had done the packing.

"Don't worry, lad. We'll start with wooden cudgels, then maybe pick up a sword along the way. I'll cut some sticks in the morning." Gawain smiled in a satisfied way, and Terence stared helplessly at the road before them.

The next morning Terence began lessons in the

broadsword, using a stout ash cudgel for a sword. For protection, he used Father La Roche's indecent shield, which Gawain had brought so that no one would find it left behind and tell Sir Lancelot, but it was unwieldy and vibrated terribly when hit. When Terence complained, Gawain tried it and proclaimed it useless. After that, Terence defended himself only with his cudgel and found that he got on much better. As Gawain had predicted, years of watching swordplay had given Terence a natural eye and instinctive reactions. His only weakness—or so Gawain said—was an unwillingness to attack. Finally, Gawain dropped his sword arm after a stroke and left Terence a wide opening. Terence made no move. "Look here, Terence," Gawain said, stopping, "you can't afford to let openings like that pass by."

Terence stepped prudently out of Gawain's reach and said, "How do I know you weren't setting a trap for me?"

"Nobody sets a trap that obvious. You could have thumped me a good one."

Terence took a breath. "But I don't want to thump you a good one, milord. I don't want to thump you at all."

Gawain looked at him curiously. "Not even to see if you could?"

"Why would I care if I could do something that I don't want to do to begin with?"

"All right. So you don't want to thump me. But what if I were someone else?"

"Who, for instance?"

"Who would you like to thump?"

"How about Guinevere?" Terence asked hopefully.

"Terence, you can't go around thumping women. Especially her."

"There, you see? What's the sense of being a knight? I have to thump the people I don't want to thump, and I can't thump the people who would really be better off for a good thumping."

"How about Sir Lancelot? You'd like to thump him, wouldn't you?"

Terence thought about this. "No, I'd like to hang him by his toes over the edge of the North Tower."

Gawain paused, struck by this. "In a cold wind?"

"In armor, without underclothes," Terence added.

Gawain's lips quivered, but he pressed on. "But wouldn't you like to thump him too?"

"While he's hanging helpless like that? Certainly not! Wouldn't be chivalrous."

"No, I mean if you couldn't hang him by his toes, wouldn't you like to thump him instead?"

"Well, it won't be the same, but I suppose I could give it a go."

"Good. Pretend that I'm Sir Lancelot."

"What? You? Impossible. Your clothes are muddy. And there's no lace on your shirt."

"Terence, I only mean —"

"And couldn't you wear a feather somewhere? In your belt or braided through your hair maybe?"

"Terence —" Gawain shook his head in amused exasperation and covered his eyes with his left hand.

Terence thumped him. "Take that, Sir Lancelot, thou recreant knight," he said.

A week later, in the woods near the village of Lowchres, Gawain and Terence came upon the first knight they had seen in almost a month. He sat on horseback at a crossroads, wearing spotless armor with a bright sash wound around the waist. He raised his lance in what could have been either a challenge or a greeting.

"Hello, sir knight," Gawain hailed him, assuming it was a greeting.

"You shall not pass, O knight," the knight replied.

"Challenge," Terence muttered.

"Very well, I won't," Gawain said pleasantly. "I only want some information. Have you ever heard of a knight clad all in green who lives at one Green Chapel?"

The knight hesitated, then said, "Don't you want to pass?"

"Only if that is the way to the Green Chapel. Do you know?"

"Sir knight," the knight said haughtily, "perhaps you do not realize it, but I have offered you a challenge."

"Yes, but I declined it."

"Then I call you a coward."

"All right. Have you heard of this knight or his chapel?"

"Why should I tell a coward anything?"

"Pity?" Gawain suggested innocently.

"Cowards are fit only to be thrashed!" the knight declared, booting his horse to a gallop. "Prepare to battle!"

"I don't have a lance," Gawain said calmly.

The knight checked abruptly, almost falling from his saddle. When he had gotten his horse under control again, he said, "I crave your pardon, sir knight. I was almost guilty of a grave discourtesy. I shall use my sword." He dropped his lance, drew his sword, and charged again. Gawain looked away.

"Milord," Terence said, "he's going to—" Gawain still made no move. Terence spurred his horse forward into the knight's path. The knight's horse, already skittish, reared, and the knight grabbed frantically at his saddle with his left hand, dropping his reins. With his cudgel, Terence landed a numbing blow on the fingers of the knight's right hand. The knight yelped and dropped his sword. Then Terence thumped the knight solidly on the side of the helm. The blow was hard enough to dent the iron, and with a groan the knight dropped his sword and fell slowly backwards from his saddle.

"Terence, you idiot!" Gawain shouted, galloping up. "What are you doing?"

Terence looked at the fallen knight and said meekly, "I thought you were just going to let him hit you."

"Well, I wasn't! You ought to be confined, rushing an armed man like that without any armor!"

"What were you going to do then?" Terence demanded.

Gawain looked at the knight, who was starting to stir weakly. "About what you did," Gawain said with a slow grin. "Well done, lad." Terence blushed, and the knight groaned. "Here, you ride over there a bit, and I'll see if I can't patch things up."

Gawain dismounted and knelt over the knight, saying, "Oh dear, I was afraid he would do something like that. Sir knight? Can you hear me?" The knight mumbled something that Terence couldn't hear, and Gawain said, "Oh good. The last knight he smote couldn't speak for weeks. Tell me, sir knight, how are you called?"

"I am Sir Oneas of Mercia, called the Knight of the Crossroads," the knight said. Gawain unlaced Sir Oneas's helm and pulled it off. Terence sneaked a quick glance, and saw that Sir Oneas was little more than a youth, probably a year or two younger than he was himself.

"Well, Sir Oneas, you are very fortunate that Sir Gawain chose not to kill you." Terence blinked but kept his face impassive.

"Sir...Sir Gawain? Of Arthur's court?" Sir Oneas asked dazedly. "You mean that's the great Sir Gawain?"

"Himself," Gawain said, with reverence. "Few are the knights who can challenge that great warrior." Terence coughed modestly.

"Sir Gawain! But...he looks so young! And why does he wear no armor?"

"Ssh! He does not choose to talk about it, but it's to fulfill a vow."

"I see," said Sir Oneas, who clearly did not.

"We had best leave you now," Gawain said. "But before we leave, perhaps you should tell Sir Gawain if you've heard of this Green Knight he seeks."

"I...no, not exactly. Unless he means the Huntsman of Anglesey."

"The Huntsman of Anglesey?"

"Due north, on the island of Anglesey. It is a fearsome adventure by all accounts." There was a pause, then Sir Oneas added, "Sir? If you think it would be all right, would you tell Sir Gawain that it was an honor to cross swords with him?"

"I shall tell him, Sir Oneas," Gawain said as he

mounted. He trotted to where Terence waited, and they rode away. Gawain chuckled. "'Cross swords' indeed. By the time he's finished with that story, I'll bet he will have fought the noble Sir Gawain for hours before he was narrowly defeated."

"Unless he says he defeated Sir Gawain," Terence said wryly. "One lie is as believable as another."

"So it is," Gawain said with a broad grin.

Gawain had kept Sir Oneas's lance, and as they rode north he began to instruct Terence in the art of jousting. First they adjusted Gawain's armor to fit Terence's much slimmer build. Then Terence had to learn how to ride while wearing armor and carrying a heavy lance. He much preferred swordplay to jousting, but he stuck to it for Gawain's sake, and after a few days was at least able to stay in the saddle and hold the lance straight.

They stopped for a time at a broad meadow so that Terence could practice tilting. On the third day, Terence was practicing alone while Gawain hunted in the forest for an ash tree with which they could make another lance when a knight appeared at the edge of the woods. The stranger was dressed all in black armor, with his visor down, and he held a long lance.

"Good day, Sir Knight," Terence said, wishing Gawain were near.

"Good day," the stranger replied in a husky voice. "I see you practicing. Would you care to try a pass with me?"

It was what Terence had feared, but the knight's tone was pleasant, and Terence grinned suddenly. "Why not?" he said and took his position across the meadow.

It was over suddenly and ignominiously for Terence. He aimed his lance straight for the stranger knight's breastplate, but the knight seemed to catch Terence's lance with his own and to push the point forcefully down toward the ground. Terence was dimly aware that he had just witnessed a superlative bit of jousting, and then his lance hit the ground, and he was jolted back out of his horse's saddle. "Let go of the lance, boy," the knight shouted, but it was too late. Terence's lance shattered under his weight, and Terence landed on his face.

He rolled over and sat up amid the splinters of his lance as the stranger rode up beside him. Terence began to laugh. "I've never seen anything like it!" Terence declared, removing Gawain's helmet.

The stranger chuckled. "That's why it worked. The best fighter is not the one who does the expected most skillfully. The best fighter is the one who takes the rest by surprise. In a joust, no one expects to have his lance knocked away. It might even surprise your master, Terence."

Terence blinked. "You know us, sir?" The knight raised his visor. It was King Arthur himself. "My liege!"

"Don't give me away, will you?" Arthur said, smiling guiltily. "The court thinks I'm having one of my retreats at that monastery. The abbot there is a friend of mine and he lets me slip out incognito."

"Is this what you always do during those weeks?"

Arthur nodded. "As king, I cannot take part in tournaments. So I stage my own, anonymously. Perhaps it's childish, but I feel better after I've bashed a few knights off their horses."

"Happy to be of service," Terence muttered. "But what if you were bashed off a horse yourself?"

Arthur shook his head. "I've never seen a knight who could," he said simply. "But enough of me. How is your search coming?"

"We've found no one who knows the Green Chapel. Right now we're off to Anglesey, where there's supposed to be some sort of supernatural huntsman."

The king lowered his visor and said, "Go with God, then. And Terence? No one else knows where I am."

"I won't tell," Terence assured him, and Arthur rode away.

A few minutes later Gawain appeared. "I can't find a tree for another lance," he announced.

"Pity," Terence said, standing amid the splinters. "I think this one's used up."

At the fishing village of Caernarvon, built on the site of an old fortress, they found a squat, vile-smelling fisherman who was willing to ferry them and their horses across to the island of Anglesey. On the way, Gawain talked to the fisherman, and when they arrived, Gawain told Terence, "If half the stories about this Huntsman of Anglesey are true, then he's a terror all right. Maybe we've found him."

"Wonderful," Terence said dully.

"Anyway," Gawain continued, "the fisherman said that we should see the Earl of Anglesey, whose castle should be just over that rise."

The Earl of Anglesey was just as squat and almost as vile-smelling as the fisherman, and his castle reeked of fish. As soon as he heard who his visitor was and that Gawain was looking for the Huntsman of Anglesey, he welcomed them with open arms and ushered them into a long hall with several ragged chairs and a roaring fire. "Oy, a bane to all decent men and women in the land, this Huntsman is," he said. "He's a terrible fierce fighter and a very demon at archery."

"Archery?" Gawain asked.

The earl nodded expressively. "That's the worst of him. That's how he's killed the most of his victims.

My own youngest son died by the Huntsman's bow, just over a year ago."

"I'm sorry to hear it," Gawain said.

The earl shrugged. "He was a wastrel, but there it is. That was what started it all. The fellow's been ravaging the countryside ever since."

"If it's not too painful, could you tell me how it happened?" Gawain asked.

"Nay, not so painful. I've got four other sons. Of course they're all wastrels, too, but there it is. Let me get you a tot of something to warm you, and I'll tell you how it was." He poured out a cup of some black liquid that Gawain sipped gingerly. "Now, where shall I begin? My son, Erkin, and his brother was out in the forests about a year ago when they come on a deer trail. Naturally they begin chasing it down, even though they doesn't even have a good deerhound along. Hunting boar, you see."

"So they didn't even have longbows with them?" Gawain asked with surprise.

"Nay, just boar spears." The earl chuckled. "I see what you're thinking. You're thinking they was all about in their heads if they thought they would bag them a deer with boar spears. Well, you're right. Proper sapskulls they are, all my sons. Blamed if I understand it. Anyway, they finally catch sight of the deer and go chasing it through the woods on their horses. So," the earl continued, "there they was, carousing through the woods after this buck when of a sudden Erkin flips right off his horse. Barzil, my other son, stops right there, thinking Erkin has run into a branch or something, which it's a wonder they hadn't, but when he looks closer he sees an arrow right through Erkin's heart. Then he hears this ferocious voice shout, 'Got you, lad! You'll make a month of dinners for me!' Well, Barzil got no more brains than a hedgehog, but he knows what's due his brother, so he remembers to pack Erkin on the back of his horse before he takes himself off."

"You say that the voice said your son would make a month of dinners?"

"Oy, that's what he said. Of course the story gets around, like they do, and people starts taking care they doesn't go too far into the deepest forest, but things still happens. A man from the east shore disappears and only his hands and feet is found, right in the middle of the forest. People sees the Huntsman himself stalking at night, and some says they've seen him, a-riding a stag the size of a horse, with antlers that reach to the sky."

Gawain nodded encouragingly. When the earl seemed to have finished, he said, "I thank you. If you'll point my way to the deepest forest, I'll see how this Huntsman likes being hunted."

In less than an hour they were in a forest so thick that only the occasional shaft of sunlight challenged the darkness. Terence had never been in a forest like it. He was not at all pleased with the prospect of sharing that darkness with a man-eating archer either, and he said so to Gawain.

"I wouldn't worry about it," Gawain said. "I've heard tales of man-eaters before, but I never found one that was true. It's the kind of story that people tell. There are monsters in this world, to be sure, but there are a sight more storytellers. Besides, you're the best archer I've ever seen. I'm depending on you to protect me."

"And who's going to protect me, then?" Terence muttered.

They made camp in a tiny clearing surrounded by huge trees hung all over with vines. Terence made a small fire, and they stretched out in the shallow pool of light and warmth near it and went to sleep. Only a few hours later, a slight stirring from the brush woke him. His eyes flew open, and he looked at Gawain over the still glowing coals. Gawain too was awake. He nodded, and Terence slipped out of his blankets and into the thickest part of the undergrowth.

Soon Terence heard the rustling again, and he crept closer. As his eyes grew accustomed to the darkness, he made out a patch of deeper darkness, roughly the size and shape of a small man. Terence breathed more easily; the Huntsman was supposed to be huge. The shape moved toward their camp, and Terence followed silently. When the shape reached the edge of the brush, it reached behind him in a move that Terence recognized at once as reaching for arrows. Terence's heart leaped, and he threw himself into the shape's back, just as the shape grunted and doubled over. Gawain stood up from his blankets, brandishing his cudgel.

"Don't move if you want your skull in one piece," Gawain said. The figure gasped and tried vainly to speak. Gawain must have hit him in the stomach.

"Are you the Huntsman of Anglesey?" Gawain asked him. The figure croaked again, something that sounded like, "Nose a king. Nose a parson." Whatever it was, it did not sound very complimentary, and Terence picked his own cudgel out of his gear. Gawain waited a second, then asked again, "Are you the one called the Huntsman of Anglesey?"

The gasping figure took several shallow breaths, then said, "An't you a bit old to be believin' sich rot? Boggart tales for the kiddies!"

Gawain grinned. "Are they? I heard these tales first from a knight, then from a fisherman, then from an earl. They didn't think they were telling ghost stories."

"Passel of fools. There's nown who hunts these woods but I meself, an honest woodsman."

Gawain nodded and said, "And what might you be called, honest woodsman?"

"I'm Dirk. I live at the edge of the woods hard by Holyhead."

"And you hunt these woods, Dirk? For your food?"

"Oy, and fish, too, in the summer. I've a boat."

"I take it, then, that you've never seen a huge black Huntsman who rides a stag with antlers that reach to the heavens?" Gawain asked solemnly.

Dirk looked exasperated. "Didn't I say there was no sich thing and no sich person? It's a tale the villagers tell to keep the kiddies out of the woods."

"Then why did you sneak up on our camp with an arrow notched?" Terence demanded.

"I'll tell you why, lad. Because ever since the earl's started telling his boggart tales, there's been no end of idiot knights—boys, most of 'em—traipsing in here frightening away the game. Last time one of 'em saw me he tried to take my head off with his sword. It an't safe for an honest man to hunt, it an't."

"How did you escape?" Gawain asked, interested.

"Stupid boy missed me and stuck his sword in a tree. Last time I passed, it was still there."

Gawain chuckled but said, "Why do you think the earl has started telling these tales, then?"

Dirk looked at his feet and said, "How'm I supposed to know what goes on in an earl's head? They be smarter than us poor folks."

"It won't go, Dirk. I've been with you only two minutes, and I already know that you're smarter than that earl. Remember, you called him a fool yourself earlier."

Dirk grinned slightly for a second, then looked away again. "I still don't know," he said.

"I think you do," Gawain said. Dirk looked at him sharply, and Gawain said, "Oh, don't worry. If it's as I think it is, I won't say anything to the earl." They were silent for a second, then Gawain said, "You killed his son, didn't you?" Dirk was glumly silent. "By mistake. You thought you had a deer, food for a good month. Then you saw what you had done, and you hid and waited until the earl's other son piled the body on his horse. Then you went home. Is that right?" Dirk looked searchingly into Gawain's eyes, then nodded.

"So there is no Huntsman of Anglesey?" Terence asked.

"Sure there is, Terence—just not the sort you were expecting. He's just a woodsman, like you."

"So we've been wasting our time," Terence said, disgusted.

"Maybe not," Gawain said. He turned back to

Dirk and said, "So your life has been miserable ever since this Huntsman story got about?" Dirk nodded. "Maybe we can help."

"How's that?"

"What do you think would do to stop the story?"

Dirk snorted. "Maybe if you killed every man, woman, and child on the island, you could stop it, but I misdoubt it."

"Nay, that would only make it worse. I've a better plan than that. I'll kill the Huntsman."

Dirk stiffened and said, "Thank 'ee kindly, your worship, but I'd rather live with the story."

Gawain ignored him and turned to Terence, "Now what do you think it would take to kill the dreadful Huntsman of Anglesey?"

Terence caught on. "How about a charmed arrow, milord?"

"That's good. How was it charmed? Should this be a religious arrow?"

"Why not?" Terence said.

"Why not indeed? Then let us say that it was charmed by the blood of St. Sebastian. Yes, that'll do. Probably the only thing in the world that would kill this ferocious beast."

"And we carried it in a silken wrap," Terence contributed.

"Good," Gawain said. He turned to Dirk. "Now,

what did the Huntsman look like? You're the only witness, so it had best be your own description."

"I'm the only witness?" Dirk began, brows knit.

"That's right. You were hunting at the edge of the forest when you heard the sound of the battle and you saw me fighting the Huntsman. What did he look like?"

"Oy, he was awful big," Dirk said, eyes wide. "An' he had hair all over his legs—I'm not so sure that he didn't have the legs of a goat, now I think on it—an' horns that looked sharp as a knife. Fearsome."

Gawain laughed with delight and said, "You're right! I remember it clearly! The legs of a goat!"

"And horns," Terence reminded him. "Sharp horns."

"An' beside him was a stag, bigger than any horse, an' it had long an' twisty prongs—snakes! It had snakes growing out of its head!"

"Don't you think it was breathing fire, too?" Gawain hinted.

"Now I think on it, it was. An' smokin' from the ears."

"Fearsome," Terence murmured.

"And what happened after I shot it with the charmed arrow?" Gawain asked.

Dirk look puzzled. "It fell down dead, of course."

"Where's its body, then?"

"Oy, I see. I mean that it started to bleed, and its blood was as red as fire — I mean its blood was fire. There was the fire of Hell in its veins, an' as soon as that charmed arrow from St. S. . . ."

"Sebastian," Gawain said. "You better say it yourself, so you can remember."

"Sebastian," Dirk repeated. "Anyway, as soon as that charmed arrow from St. Sebastian touched it, fire come out in a rush and burned it and the stag right up."

"Well done," Gawain said approvingly. "Then I saw you, and introduced myself to you — How do you do? I am Sir Gawain of King Arthur's Round Table."

"Are you really?" Dirk asked. "From the Round Table?"

"I really am. I introduced myself to you — How do you do? and so on — and told you that that had been an arrow of St. Sebastian's, and told you to build a shrine on that spot."

"Do I have to build the shrine for real?"

"You won't need to. The villagers will do it. And then I left, with my faithful squire by my side. You have all that?"

"St. Sebastian, Sir Gawain, King Arthur, a shrine," Dirk said. "Will they believe me?"

"It was a story that started all this. Why shouldn't another end it?"

Terence coughed gently. "Milord, don't you think that a good shrine ought to have a religious relic? Like maybe an image of—"

Gawain burst into approving laughter. "Go get it, lad."

Terence fetched Father La Roche's shield. Gawain handed it reverently to Dirk. "This," he said, "is the magical shield which protected me from the unnatural darts of the cruel Huntsman."

Dirk repeated this to himself with obvious pleasure. "I like that," he said. "'Unnatural darts.' What's this on the inside?" He held the shield up to the light to look at the painting.

Gawain cleared his throat and said, "Before you say anything, you should know that that's the Blessed Virgin."

"Just coming out of her bath, is she?" Dirk asked.

"Just put it in the shrine," Gawain said, grinning. "Terence? Get our gear together." Terence started to pack their traps, and Gawain turned back to Dirk. "And Dirk? Have you ever heard of a knight colored all in green? Or a place called the Green Chapel?"

"Should I put them in the tale, too, do you think?"

"Nay, Dirk. These are real. Do you know them?"

Dirk shook his head. "We've nothing like that on the island. They've got some real knights in the Wilderness of Wirral, east of Caernarvon, though. You might ask them."

V

THE WILDERNESS
OF WIRRAL

The Wilderness of Wirral was only forty miles from
Caernarvon, just north of the town of Chester, and
Gawain and Terence arrived by early afternoon.
Despite its ominous-sounding name, it was really a
pleasant little wood. They made camp by a chuckling brook, and Terence took his bow into the woods
to hunt up some dinner. Before long he spotted several rabbit holes. He made himself comfortable and
waited for the rabbits to come out for their evening
feeding. In about an hour, an enormous rabbit poked
his head out of the nearest hole and stared hard at
the bush where Terence was hiding.

"Oh dear, oh dear," the rabbit said. "There's a
nasty hunter, planning to eat me and my family for
his dinner. Whatever shall I do?"

Terence grinned. "Robin?" he said.

Years earlier, on the day that Terence had first met Gawain, Terence had also encountered a mischievous elf named Robin, a sort of messenger between the World of Men and the Other World. In fact, Robin had led Terence to Gawain. Although Robin had made game of Terence more than once, Terence was fond of the sprite, who was his most frequent contact with the faery realm.

The rabbit chuckled, then began to stretch, growing taller and changing form. In a moment the little green elf stood before him. "Hallo, Terence."

"Well, where have you been keeping yourself?" Terence said, striding forward. "I haven't seen you in ages."

"Oh, here and there," the sprite said, waving his arm vaguely. "You?"

"Questing again, as I suppose you know."

"Ay, that I do. That's why I'm here."

Terence nodded. "You have a message for Gawain?"

"Nay, young master. A message for you. If your quest is to go on, it depends on you, not Gawain."

"What do you mean?" Terence frowned.

"You didn't sleep well last night, did you?"

"We didn't sleep at all. We were...we were busy fighting a terrible Huntsman."

"Were you then?" Robin asked, eyes twinkling. "And did you use a charmed arrow and a magic

shield with the true face of the Blessed Virgin on it?"
Terence blinked, and Robin added, "Nay, don't be
surprised, lad. It's all over the countryside. There's
already a group of pilgrims forming in Chester to go
view the scene of your battle. But whatever you did
last night, it left your master sleepy, and when you
went out hunting he lay down for a nap."

"So?"

"It was how he got captured."

"*What?*"

"By the Marquis of Alva. He's the great lord of
the lands hereabouts, and a black-hearted villain. He
hates all knights except his own, and he hates the
knights of the Round Table most of all. On feast
days he has captured knights brought out and put to
death for his amusement. And, in case it's slipped
your mind, Good Friday is five days away."

"What should I do?"

"Rescue him, of course," Robin said with surprise.

"Just like that? How do I do it?"

"Come now, young master. You know I only tell
you what to do, never how to do it. But—" Robin
paused, as if in thought— "I understand that the
marquis has recently misplaced his underchef, and
with the feast coming up is in need of some kitchen
help." Terence nodded eagerly; he had been cook-
ing all his life, first for the Hermit, then for Gawain.

82

Robin produced two packets, one small and one quite large. "Here are two powders. The white powder in the small bag is tasteless, and when just a pinch is mixed with a person's food, that person will sleep like a baby for hours. The yellow powder is a powerful spice, from far away to the east, sure to disagree with any true Englishman's digestion."

Terence took the packets and asked, "Where do I find this Marquis of Alva?"

"Do you see that rabbit?" Robin pointed at a rabbit coming out of another hole. "Follow it, and it will take you to the Chateau Wirral, the seat of the Marquis of Alva." The rabbit saw Terence and bolted. Terence started, then dived frantically into the brush after it. Behind him, Robin called, "Run fast!"

It was just like Robin to have him chasing a rabbit instead of something a bit slower, Terence thought between breaths. He ran as fast as he could, gasping for air, losing sight of the rabbit every ten steps or so but always spotting it again. He leaped over rocks and bushes that he would never have tried to jump before, and he fell only three or four times. His throat began to burn, and his chest ached with every breath, but he didn't slow down until he ran headlong into a large grey stallion with a woman on its back.

Terence tried to dodge, but he still hit the horse a glancing blow on its shoulder and sprawled in the dirt.

"You idiot! You cabbageheaded domnoddy! If you've hurt my horse, I'll have your skin!" the rider shouted shrilly.

Terence scrambled to his feet, wheezing, and managed to mutter, "Beg pardon ma'am," between gasps, and looked frantically around for the rabbit. It was gone.

"Look at me, boy!" the rider demanded.

Terence obeyed and saw that she was only a girl, maybe sixteen. "Have you...seen a rabbit...go by here?"

She stared. "Are you chasing a rabbit on foot? How stupid!"

"Hurry, girl! Did you see it?" Terence demanded impatiently.

Her mouth dropped open, and with a stunned look on her face, she pointed north. Terence wasted no more time but wheeled and started running again. Behind him the girl shouted, "Hey! Stop there, you boy!" but Terence ignored her. Soon he spied the rabbit again, and then they both burst out of the woods. Terence slowed to a stop and stared at the Chateau Wirral, rising incongruously out of the forest.

It was an ancient-looking fortress, squat and dark

and thick-walled. The keep, a circular stone tower in the center of the fortress, rose high above the walls, but nothing else interrupted the long, level line of stone. The gate stood open, but two guards armed with battle-axes stood on either side of the entrance. Terence caught his breath, then strolled forward, whistling.

"You, there!" one of the guards called to him. "What's your business, eh?"

"I've got no business at all," Terence replied mournfully. "And no food in my gut because of it."

"Well, clear off. We've no food for beggers here."

"I'm no begger!" Terence declared, offended. "I'm a squire, I am." He rubbed his nose with the back of his hand.

The guards laughed, and one of them said, "Ho! A squire, it is. Don't you mean a knight? D'you think we should bow before Sir Sniffles here?"

Terence grinned sheepishly. "Well, almost a squire anyway. I would have been, but the knight what would have taken me on was popped off in a tourney. Does the guv'nor here need a squire?"

"Clear off, boy," one of the guards said, smiling in a kind way. "You don't want to work here. Go hunting with that bow of yours."

Terence had forgotten the bow slung over his shoulder. "But I'm no good with it, you see. Are you sure there's no need for a squire? You see, I don't want to go back to work in the kitchens unless I has to. I'd be a good squire."

The other guard, whose face was sharper than his companion's, said, "The kitchens, eh? A serving-lad?"

"What, a scruff-boy? I should say not! I'm a cook, I am — but I'd rather be a squire."

"A cook, eh? Well, the lord here might have some use for you, after all."

The kindly guard said, "Forget it, Glynn. This here's a good lad, and he don't want to work in the marquis's kitchens. Go on to Chester, boy, and find work there, right?"

Terence started to argue, but before he could speak, a dark, heavy-browed man in a dirty velvet blouse appeared in the gate. "What's this, guards? Chitter-chatter? Who's this vermin?" he demanded. Both guards went rigid, and their faces became blank, as if all expression had been wiped away with a cloth. The heavy-browed man asked again, "Who is this peasant brat?"

The second guard, Glynn, said, "A boy seeking a position in the kitchens, my lord."

"Actually, I'd like to be a squire—" Terence began, playing his part to the end, but the kindly guard gave him a sharp warning look, and Terence stopped.

"If I take you on, you'll learn to speak when

spoken to, or you'll learn to live with no skin on your back," the man said. He looked at Terence thoughtfully. "Can you cook?"

"Yes, sir."

"Yes what?"

"Yes...my lord?"

"Hmm. What's your best dish?"

"Roast capons with mushrooms, my lord. Or broiled trout in wine sauce."

The marquis grunted, then nodded. "Right. You're on. But none of those fancy dishes, mind." He looked at the two guards, then said, "The dumbhead on the right. Take him to the kitchens." Then, as suddenly as he had appeared, he vanished.

"Cor," Terence said after a moment. "Is he always like that? Popping up then popping out?"

Neither guard replied. Glynn said, "Keep a civil tongue in your head. Follow me."

The kitchens were large and busy, but Terence, used to dealing with Camelot's huge kitchen court, soon knew his way around tolerably well. He barely had time to leave his bow and arrows in a dry corner before the surly chief cook set him to work stirring a cauldron of gruel for the yeoman soldiers and another of thin barley soup for the castle servants. Both were unappetizing in the extreme, and Terence pitied those who were to eat them. He wondered which of the various doorways led to the dungeons where he could check on Gawain, but he realized that he could not simply ask. He would have to explore later.

"Boy!" the chief cook shouted.

It occurred to Terence that no one had ever asked his name. Indeed, as as long as he had been in the Chateau Wirral only the kindly guard at the gate had used a person's name. "Yes, sir?"

"Sweep that muck over there into a bucket." The cook pointed to the bones and entrails that had been cast onto the floor. "The dungeon guards will come get it when they're ready."

Terence stared. "You mean that's for the prisoners? No one could eat that mess!"

The cook chuckled in a grunty way. "That's their lookout, eh?"

An hour or so later, a guard came to get the swill bucket. He looked at the contents, then laughed and asked if the cook had anything to foul it up a bit. The cook leaned over the bucket and spat into it. "There you go, guard. Now mix that in, see, so that the whole bucket's flavored." Terence could only stare. Was no one in this place human? The guard retreated down the hallway, chuckling.

Finally the cook sent Terence to bed and, since Terence had come straight from the gate to the kitchens, gave him directions to the servants' quarters. Terence listened to these directions with only half his attention because even though he was desperately tired, he had no intention of sleeping until he had found Gawain. As soon as the cook's back was turned, he slipped down the hallway that the dungeon guard had taken.

Soon he was hopelessly lost among the black hallways of the castle and was cursing himself for not remembering a candle. After perhaps an hour of running into walls, he saw a glimmer of light around a corner. He headed toward it, hoping that it was a torch he could borrow. He turned the corner and almost ran into a girl carrying a candle.

"Excuse me, ma'am," Terence muttered, eyes down.

"Oaf!" the girl said. "What are you doing in this hallway?"

"I'm new, ma'am," Terence said. "I got lost."

"You!" the girl exclaimed suddenly. Terence looked up and groaned inwardly. "You're the ill-mannered boy who ran into me in the forest!"

"Yes, ma'am. I'm sorry, ma'am."

"Why wouldn't you stop when I called?" she demanded. "I ought to have you beaten for impudence!"

Terence blinked and looked up. The girl was short and sturdy, and her nose turned up sharply. Had she been smiling, it might have been a pleasant face, but at the moment she looked like a child having a tantrum. Terence said, "Well, of all the mean-spirited little cats! I'd like to know what harm I did you or that horse of yours. And what's more, this afternoon in the forest I wasn't a servant here, so why the devil should I have obeyed you anyway?" The girl's eyes widened with shock, and Terence bit his tongue. Getting himself thrown into the dungeons would not help Gawain. "I beg your pardon, ma'am."

"You insolent cub!" she said. "I'll have your skin for this!"

That was it then. The girl would call the guard, and Terence would never be able to hide in a strange castle for long. Furious with himself, Terence snapped, "Go ahead, then. Have me beaten, if it gives you pleasure. It probably will, if you're like everyone else in this castle. But you'll have to catch me."

Terence turned sharply, but the girl called, "Wait!" and he hesitated. In a voice that throbbed with emotion, the girl said, "I'm *not* like the rest! I'm not! Here, take this candle and go." She whirled around and stalked with dignity through a nearby doorway.

Surprised but relieved, Terence took the candle and continued his search. With the light from the candle, it was much easier to get his bearings, and soon he found the dungeons, at the foot of a long, winding stairway. Terence listened and heard at least three guards talking about the "fancy new knight"; then he crept upstairs and through a door to the outer court. Smelling the unmistakable aroma of a stable, Terence decided not to bother looking for the servants' quarters. He slipped into the stable and burrowed into the straw to sleep for a few hours.

He was awakened by something cold and wet against his cheek. He rolled his head away and opened his eyes. Through a grey morning light, he saw the outline of Gawain's horse Guingalet, standing over him and nuzzling his face.

Terence scrambled backward, crablike, out of range of Guingalet's wicked teeth, but the horse simply followed. Slowly Terence stood, then tentatively patted Guingalet's neck. "Hel...hello, old boy. Good to see you." Guingalet did not take offense at being addressed so familiarly, and Terence breathed more easily. Terence glanced around. Nearby was Terence's own horse, and on a table toward the back wall Terence recognized their saddles and packs. It looked as if everything but Gawain's sword and armor was there. Guingalet rubbed his head against Terence's chest, and Terence patted the horse's shoulder. "Here now, boy. What's this?" His fingers had run across something dry and rough caked to Guingalet's shoulder. "Have you hurt yourself, boy?"

"It's not the horse's blood," said a female voice a few yards away. Terence jumped with fear and squinted into the darkness. A second later, the girl who had given him the candle stepped into the light coming through the door. "He bit one of the grooms," the girl explained. "He's a very fierce animal. Or at least he was yesterday."

Terence swallowed and said, "I've always been good with horses, ma'am."

"A miracle worker, more like," she said. "Unless, of course, he knows you."

"Oh no, ma'am," Terence protested.

"Where *were* you off to in such a hurry yesterday?"

"Like you said, ma'am. Hunting."

"I don't believe you. And what were you looking for last night in the halls?"

"The servants' quarters, ma'am."

"I don't believe you. And what are you doing down here at this hour?"

"Why the devil should I tell you if you're not going to believe me?" Terence snapped. As before, the girl seemed astonished at Terence's forthrightness. "For that matter," Terence continued, "what are *you* doing in the stables so early?"

The girl stammered, "It's the only time when I can get.... Who are you to be asking questions of me?"

"For that matter, who are you to be asking ques-

92

tions of me?" Terence countered, adding as an afterthought, "though it's not likely that anyone in this blighted place would actually tell her name."

"My name is Lady Eileen," the girl said defiantly. "I'm the niece of the marquis."

"Oh, I suppose that's why you think that everyone is terrified of you," Terence said, nodding.

"Look here," the girl said, "I may be related to him, but I'm not like him. I hate it here. I hate this place with all my heart. I'd leave in a second if I could." She paused, panting. "Now, I've told you my name. What's yours?"

"Terence," he said. Immediately he wished he had given a false name, but it was too late.

The Lady Eileen's eyes widened. "So that's it," she said, with dawning understanding. "That new knight that my uncle brought in is Sir Gawain of the Round Table, and you're his squire!"

"Sir Who?" Terence asked, feigning bewilderment.

"Don't be an ass," the Lady Eileen said shortly. "Everyone here has heard about Sir Gawain and his squire Terence and how Sir Gawain defeated the great Sir Oneas of the Crossroads and about his mighty battle with the Huntsman of Anglesey and the new shrine of Our Lady of Anglesey."

"You've heard that already?" Terence said, caught off balance. "But it's just been two days —" He stopped abruptly.

Eileen continued, nodding to herself. "So last night you were looking for the dungeons. Did you find them?" Terence nodded. "I won't give you away," she said finally. "And I hope you free him." She turned sharply and left the stable.

"Lady Eileen?" Terence said. She stopped, and Terence said, "Thank you." She nodded curtly. "And Lady Eileen? Don't eat your dinner tonight. I'm working in the kitchens, you see."

Terence spent an exhausting but profitable day in the kitchens. The cook cursed and beat him, but he gathered some valuable information. He learned that Gawain was to be executed on Good Friday, that the marquis had a notoriously delicate digestion (trust Robin to know that), and that the marquis's dinner was to end with a bland and spongy kidney pie. When the cook stepped out of the kitchen for a minute, it was a simple matter for Terence to empty half the packet of yellow powder that Robin had given him into the kidney pie and then cover it with the top crust. The rest of the powder he poured into a large plum pudding that the cook had left him stirring.

Soon after the kidney pie was sent to the marquis's table, there was a commotion from the dining hall, and some guards came to take the cook to the marquis. Terence gathered his bow and arrows, grabbed a handful of candles, and slipped away into the maze of halls he had explored the night before. He found a secluded corner and settled down to wait for the yellow powder to have its full effect.

"Terence!" a voice whispered urgently, and something poked Terence—not gently—in the ribs. He jerked and there was the Lady Eileen standing over him holding a lamp. "Wake up."

Terence realized that he had been asleep. "What time is it?" he asked quickly.

"Just after three. What did you put in the food tonight? Everyone who ate at our table is groaning as if they were about to die." She paused, then asked, "Are they?"

"About to die?" Lady Eileen nodded. Terence shook his head doubtfully and said, "I don't know."

"I hope they do," she said fiercely. "They sawed a knight in half last Christmas. I heard them laughing about it. What are you going to do now?"

Terence found himself telling the Lady Eileen his plans. It didn't take long. When he had finished, she said, "That's it? You're going to give this other powder to the guards and put them to sleep. How?"

"I don't know," Terence admitted.

Lady Eileen thought briefly. "What you need is a bottle of wine. That's what the guards will swallow fastest."

"But where will I get a bottle of—?"

"Come with me." Lady Eileen grabbed Terence's hand and led him quickly through the halls to a bedchamber with a fire roaring in the fireplace. "Here," she said, digging into a chest full of clothes, "put these on over your clothes"— she held up an old grey dress and a red wool shawl —"and go down to the dungeons with this bottle."

"I'm not going to wear that!"

"If you go down in your own clothes, they'll probably kill you on sight," she said briskly. "Here, you'll need a corset to give you the right shape."

Terence felt himself being swept along helplessly and resented Lady Eileen's imperious planning, but after protesting once or twice more, for form's sake, he agreed. It took several minutes to dress, mostly to get the corset tightened. Soon, though, Terence was awkwardly descending the dungeon steps, the bottle in one hand and the hem of his dress in the other.

"Who goes there?" a gruff voice asked.

"Is this the Lady Eileen's room?" Terence asked in a quavering falsetto. "Oh, dear, I must be lost, and Lady Eileen waiting for this wine."

"Hey, fellows!" the gruff voice said. "It's a woman! And she has wine!"

Terence gave a flustered squawk and fell over backwards, gently setting the bottle of wine on the stone floor. Then he picked up his skirts and ran back up the stairs as fast as he could. Behind him he heard the guard laugh raucously and call out that the wench had dropped her wine. Ten minutes later, still in his feminine disguise, Terence peeked around the corner. Three guards lay sprawled in an untidy heap on the floor, breathing deeply and evenly.

"Milord!" Terence called out.

"Terence?" Gawain's muffled voice came from the end of a dark passageway.

"Wait there, milord!" Terence hurried down the hall and drew the bolt on the last door. Scruffy and stained but uninjured, Gawain stepped out.

"Very fetching," Gawain said. "The grey dress brings out your eyes."

Terence ignored him. "Here," he said, handing Gawain a lamp and stripping off the dress and shawl. "Stop laughing like a half-wit and help me with this corset. Are there any other prisoners here?"

"Nay, lad. I'm the only one. Just in time for the Good Friday feast, too. Everyone seems to think it's a stroke of luck. How did you get into this thing? I thought it was hard to put on armor!"

When Terence at last stood free of his disguise, he led Gawain back up the stairs. "The horses and our gear are in a stable just outside. If we can saddle them without being seen, we can charge right through the main gate."

"My armor? And the Sword Galatine?" Gawain asked.

Terence shook his head. Gawain stopped at the top of the stairway. "Then let's go find them. Do you know your way around this castle?"

"Milord, do you know what they plan to do to you?" Terence pleaded.

"They mentioned crucifixion," Gawain said. "Good Friday, you know. Where would be a good place to look for the armor?"

Terence knew that tone and gave up. "Follow me," he said and led Gawain back to Lady Eileen's bedchamber.

She answered the door at Terence's second knock. "What are you doing back here?" she asked, ushering them into the room. "Good evening, Sir Gawain."

"Who is this, Terence?" Gawain demanded. "I never told anyone my name."

"Why aren't you at the stables already?" Lady Eileen asked.

"Sir Gawain won't leave without his armor," Terence said to Lady Eileen.

Her eyes flashed angrily. "Well, he's a domnoddy, then!"

"Don't tell me!" Terence protested. "Tell him! And he's not either a domnoddy!"

"Pardon me, my lady—" Gawain began.

"Don't use that tone of voice with me, kitchen boy!" Lady Eileen snapped.

"I'm not a kitchen boy. I'm a squire."

"Well, you're still somebody's servant."

"Not *yours*, thank heaven," Terence retorted.

"Pardon me, my lady," Gawain said again. "But if you live in this castle, perhaps you can tell me where I might find my armor and sword."

"My uncle keeps all the armor he captures in his treasure room, and the only entrance to the treasure room is in his chamber."

"Her uncle is the marquis," Terence explained.

"And where is your uncle's chamber?" Gawain asked.

"You're not going to try to get it back!" she exclaimed.

"But of course. It's mine, you see."

"Men are such idiots!" she said, rolling her eyes.

"Just tell him where it is," Terence said. "He won't leave until you do."

"At the end of this hall is another hall. You take the turning on the...on the..." she hesitated uncertainly.

"Oh for heaven's sake, why can't women ever tell their left from their right?" Terence moaned. He gestured with his right then his left hand. "Is it this way or that way?"

"Be quiet, kitchen boy. It's this way—right. My uncle's chamber is at the end of that second hall."

"Thank you, my lady," Gawain bowed. "You wait for me here, Terence."

Before Terence could protest, Gawain was gone, running lightly down the hall. Terence looked at Lady Eileen, shrugged, and said, "Sorry. Do you mind if I sit down?"

"I don't see how I can stop you," she replied ungraciously. Terence sat. For a few seconds neither spoke, then Lady Eileen said, "I hope he kills him. I do. I do."

"Kills your uncle?"

"Yes. He's a fiend!" she said.

"True. But why aren't you like him? Growing up with him here and all."

"I didn't grow up here! My father was the marquis's younger brother, and a good man. When he died, six months ago, I came here to live with my uncle. I didn't know what he was like."

"And he took you in?"

Lady Eileen nodded. "And all my inheritance. Oh, I do hope Sir Gawain kills him."

Gawain was gone longer than expected. It was fully twenty minutes later before he walked proudly into the room wearing his armor and carrying a sword in each hand. "Sorry I was so long, Terence, but I took a few minutes choosing a good sword for you from the stock there. This looks like a fine blade."

Terence passed his hands over his eyes in anguish. "Milord, you tried to dress yourself, didn't you?"

Lady Eileen said, "You spent time in there choosing a sword for Terence?"

"What's wrong?" Gawain asked Terence. "I thought I suited up pretty well for being in the dark."

"What does a squire need with a sword?" Lady Eileen demanded.

"It's a miracle it didn't drop off you in the hallway," Terence moaned.

"Let me tell you, my lad, that I put on my armor myself for years before I met you."

"And it's a mystery to us all that you're still alive, I'm sure." Terence nodded. "Now you've got your armor back, I just hope you don't lose it."

"A bit loose is all," Gawain said. "I couldn't reach all the ties. You should sympathize, Terence. I'm sure you have the same trouble with your corset."

Lady Eileen laughed and said, "You should have seen his face when I tied that on, Sir Gawain."

"Oh, are you the one who helped him? But of course you are. I'm afraid I've forgotten my manners. I've never even asked your name."

"Lady Eileen," she said, curtsying grandly.

"Look, can we get out of here?" Terence asked.

"Charmed," Gawain said with a deep bow.

"Terence is right, Sir Gawain. You really should be leaving."

"Oh, very well," Gawain said with a polite smile. "I've had a lovely evening, my lady."

Lady Eileen giggled, and Terence rolled his eyes. They turned toward the door, but Lady Eileen asked, "Did you kill my uncle?"

"No. I had to knock him around a bit, but I didn't think it would be polite to kill him after all you've done to help." Lady Eileen slumped with disappointment, and Gawain said, "But I'd be happy to go back, if you like. The only thing is, he's not feeling well, and I don't think it's chivalrous to kill someone on the chamberpot."

"Milord, we have to leave," Terence said firmly.

Lady Eileen sighed and said, "I suppose you're right. Maybe he'll die anyway."

"He certainly sounds as though he will," Gawain said encouragingly.

"Milord!"

"Oh, all right, Terence."

Gawain led the way out of the room. As he closed the door, Terence looked back at Lady Eileen, whose face was a curious mixture of amusement and dejection. "Thank you, Lady Eileen," he said. She nodded, and then Gawain and Terence were running down the hallway, swords at the ready.

They made it to the stables without incident and hurriedly saddled their horses, but when Terence opened the stable doors again, they found a score of yeoman soldiers lined up outside, all armed with spears. At their head was the marquis himself, looking extremely unwell and very pale in the moonlight but standing nevertheless. "At them!" the marquis cried, and the line charged.

Terence dropped to one knee, slipped his bow from his shoulder, and began firing arrow after arrow into the ranks. He had never fired so swiftly, and four soldiers were down before the line of soldiers came to Gawain. Then Terence drew his new sword from its scabbard on his saddle. For the next few minutes, he did not think but only slashed and parried by instinct. To his left he heard Gawain's roaring battle cry and the dull thud-thud-thud of his master's sword on the leather uniforms of the soldiers.

A soldier's face loomed before him, and Terence drew back his arm to cut at it, but stopped. It was the kind guard from the gate, and as Terence looked into his eyes he knew in an instant, though how he could not say, that this guard would not hurt him. Terence whirled away and faced another charging soldier, but before Terence could strike, the new attacker stopped short, with the first guard's spear in his chest. Then Gawain and Terence and the guard were standing alone amid a scattering of dead and wounded.

"Thank you, friend," Terence said. The guard nodded, but looked only at his fellow-soldier whom he had killed. "My name's Terence," Terence added.

At that the guard looked up. "My name is Alan," he said. "And you can't know what a relief it is to tell someone my name."

"Can't I just? This is Sir Gawain, of King Arthur's Round Table." Alan stared at Gawain with awe, then knelt before him.

"Nay, friend. I should kneel to you, in gratitude." Gawain grasped Alan's shoulders and gently raised him. Then Gawain looked around. "Where's the marquis?"

He was not there. Alan said, "He must have gone for more men. He can get as many as fifty from the barracks."

"Long odds. Perhaps we had best leave, Terence, if you'll stop dawdling. You'll come with us, Alan?"

Alan beamed. "With pleasure, Sir Gawain. I'll get a horse." He raced back into the stable. Terence glanced up the wall of the towering keep. Outlined against a lighted window was Lady Eileen. Gawain dropped a hand on Terence's shoulder and said, "You did well, lad."

"Wait here!" Terence said abruptly. Still carrying

his sword, he ran back into the dark building, up the stairs, and down the hall to Lady Eileen's chamber. He pushed open the door without knocking and looked at her, panting from his run. She stared back but said nothing. "Come with us," he said.

"Come...I can't...I..." she stammered.

"You said you'd leave if you could. Now's your chance."

She stared at Terence for another second, then leaped into frenzied action. She grabbed a small bag and stuffed some clothes and a comb into it— of course she'd have to have a comb, Terence thought—and threw on a heavy traveling cloak. The whole process of packing took less than three minutes. They ran together down to the stable, where Terence helped her saddle the beautiful grey stallion he had seen her on before. He reached over to help her mount, but she pushed him away and climbed lightly into the saddle. Gawain, who had said nothing when he saw them come out of the tower, said pleasantly, "Shall we go then, if everyone's ready?"

They stepped out of the stables to see the marquis, clearly illuminated by the torches held by some thirty soldiers, standing between them and the main gate. Gawain rode forward and stopped, facing the line of soldiers. "My name is Sir Gawain," he said. "Are you all willing to die for your master as these others have? Do you love this cruel marquis so much?"

There was a slight rustling among the soldiers. "Attack!" shouted the marquis. No one moved.

"Come on, friends," Gawain said to Terence and the others. They trotted forward, and the line of soldiers parted for them, as if by magic.

"Attack, you craven dogs!" the marquis screamed. He saw Alan and Lady Eileen. "Traitors! Traitors! Kill them!" Still no one moved. "I'll have you all flayed!" shrieked the marquis. Without speaking, the soldiers moved in a circle until they surrounded their master.

Gawain's little cavalcade reached the gate and trotted through. A minute later, just before they entered the forest, a wild inhuman shriek rose from the castle. They stopped and looked back.

"They killed him, didn't they?" Lady Eileen said.

"Wouldn't you?" said Alan. Then they rode together into the Wilderness of Wirral.

VI

THE ELFIN VILLAGE

The sun was already past its zenith when Terence awakened in their camp in the Wilderness of Wirral. Gawain and the soldier Alan were leaning together against a tree, talking in low voices. Behind them, wrapped in one of Gawain's blankets, Lady Eileen watched them. Terence threw off his covers, and Gawain turned.

"Good afternoon, Sir Slothful," he said, smiling. "Come join me. I was just trying to convince your friend Alan to ride along with us."

"Nay, my lord," Alan said apologetically. "I've no place in adventures like yours. I'm naught but a simple soldier."

"But soldiers' lives are filled with wars and adventures," Gawain protested.

Alan shook his head, smiling. "Not a bit, my lord.

A soldier's life is filled with chores and standing guard and saving his pay for a drop of ale with his barrack mates and telling lies about adventures to the lasses. I'd never been in a battle until that little turn-up last night in the courtyard. I'm a peaceful man, all told, and I wish for a peaceful soldier's life."

Gawain chuckled and nodded. "Have you a fancy to be a soldier for King Arthur?" Alan gasped, and nodded enthusiastically. "Very well, then, you shall be. Ride to Camelot and tell them you have tidings of Sir Gawain's quest. Tell the king all that you know of our adventures in the Chateau Wirral, and don't leave out your own part. Then, ask a favor of the king for Sir Gawain—that he give the bearer of this tale a commission in his yeoman troops. I promise you that the king will grant the favor. Is that clear?"

Gawain made Alan repeat the instructions until he had them by rote. Alan tried to learn more about the escape, his part in the night's adventures having been fairly limited, but Gawain simply said that he should tell what he knew himself, and fill in whatever was needed to make it a good story. So Alan left them, and Gawain turned to Lady Eileen.

"And now, my lady, we must decide what you shall do." He smiled, and Lady Eileen nodded, her face tight. Now that she was not bossing him around, she seemed suddenly small to Terence. "What do you wish?" Gawain asked.

In a thin voice, she said, "I don't know."

"Is there somewhere we could escort you? We are yours to command." Lady Eileen shook her head. "Any other family?" She shook her head again. "Why then, you must come questing with us!" Gawain declared.

Lady Eileen smiled, uncertainly at first, then more brightly. Terence had been right: her face could be quite pleasant. Young, of course, and too many freckles, but not actually unattractive. "Do you mean it, Sir Gawain?" she asked.

"I mean it. And Terence also extends his invitation. Don't you, Terence?"

Terence shrugged and said, "If you want to."

"I think I would," she said shyly. "So long as I won't be in the way."

Gawain chuckled. "Little fear of that. You faced danger last night like a queen. Moreover, I've never seen a horsewoman with a better seat. And one of the finest horses, as well."

Lady Eileen flushed with pleasure. "His name is Caesar, and I've had him since he was a colt. He's the most wonderful horse in the world." She broke off and added anxiously, "But your horse is very nice, too, Sir Gawain."

Gawain's lips quivered only slightly as he bowed and said, "Thank you, my—"

"Guingalet is the greatest horse in all of Arthur's stables!" Terence broke in, offended.

"I said he was very nice, didn't I?" Lady Eileen snapped. "And don't interrupt people. It's rude."

"You don't have to teach me manners!" Terence replied hotly. "I've served at King Arthur's own table!"

Lady Eileen sniffed. "And don't come over high and mighty with me, Sir Terence. I've seen you in a dress."

Gawain sat on the greensward and laughed, and Terence promised himself that he would never again argue with a female.

They rested all that day and then set off the next morning, riding east. For one full day they rode up into hills, and all the next, they rode down their other side. In the hills they had seen no one, but in the valley, on the bank of a river, they came upon a woodcutter carrying a bundle of sticks, and Gawain stopped to ask his usual questions.

"A Green Chapel, you say." The woodcutter rubbed his beard. "Can't rightly say for sure, but there's a chapel along the river toward Littleborough."

"Is it green?" Gawain asked quickly. "Or called green by people?"

"Can't say what folks'm likely to call a chapel," the woodcutter said. "You said it was green?"

"No, I'm asking you. Is it green?"

"You could say that." The woodcutter nodded obligingly. "I'd call it grey, myself."

Gawain looked at him suspiciously. "Have you ever heard anyone refer to this grey chapel as the Green Chapel?"

"Nay, that would be daft, then." Gawain took a deep breath. Helpfully, the woodcutter continued, "Or then you might be meaning the other chapel, up toward Nottingham? It be grey, too, as I recall."

"Never mind," Gawain said. "Forget about chapels. Can you tell us where we might find a good ford across this river?"

"Ay, there be one by the grey chapel, so long as you're heading that way," the woodcutter said. "But you'll have to move along to get out of the forest by nightfall. Unless you go to the other grey chapel." The woodcutter nodded sagely, as if pleased to have been so much help. Lady Eileen stifled a giggle.

"Thank you for your help, friend," Gawain said, his eyes bright with amusement. "Perhaps we should look for that ford tomorrow. By the grey chapel, you said?"

Suddenly the woodcutter looked uncomfortable.

"Ay, the grey one. But you weren't planning to stay in the forest tonight, were you?"

Gawain looked at him closely. "We are. Should we not?"

"Boggarts! After dark, this whole forest is alive with them. It's unhealthful!"

"Is it, then? I thank you for your information."

The woodcutter nodded, advised them again to make haste, then shambled off to the north. Gawain turned south, and the three rode in silence along the riverbank. Finally Lady Eileen said heartily, "Silly, isn't it? All these superstitions among the peasantry."

"Not always so silly, my lady," Gawain said. "Sometimes, of course, they're just tales, but there is more in this world than any of us have ever dreamed."

"You think this forest might be haunted then?" Terence asked. He was annoyed that his own voice sounded as artificial as had Lady Eileen's.

"I hope so, Terence. Where better to seek the Green Knight than in a haunted forest?"

This was clearly unanswerable, so Terence said nothing. The sun was setting when Gawain found a spot to camp, in a perfectly circular little clearing about twenty yards from the river. Terence told himself that it was just the long shadows of sunset that made the clearing look stark and forbidding, but he couldn't help feeling that they were in some sort of uncanny place, a place where something hidden took place and where they were not welcome. Gawain stepped away from Lady Eileen, beside Terence.

"Terence?" he whispered. "You've more faery blood than I. Do you feel something about this clearing?" Terence nodded. "Things happen here, don't they?"

Terence nodded again. "Not good things."

"Are we in danger?"

"I don't know, milord. I'm afraid of this place, but not that kind of afraid. Not afraid of danger."

Gawain looked pensively at Lady Eileen for a moment, then said, "We'll stay here tonight. If anything happens, leave it to me. You take care of Eileen. All right?" Terence looked at Lady Eileen, without much confidence. Gawain laid his hand on Terence's shoulder and said, "Believe me, lad. In this place, you're far more protection for her than I am." He went to groom their horses while Terence cooked dinner.

That night Terence closed his eyes and rolled up in his blankets, but he had never felt less like sleeping. His vague sense of unease had deepened with the darkness. Lady Eileen slept peacefully on the other side of the fire, and Gawain sat at the foot of a tree, still in his armor, holding the Sword Galatine, watching the night.

After perhaps an hour, Terence heard something, not a noise so much as a disturbance in the familiar noises, as if a pocket of silence were moving toward them. A violent chill quivered up Terence's spine and tickled his scalp. The stillness approached, then stopped. Gawain gasped softly, and his eyes widened. Terence followed Gawain's gaze and saw a girl.

She was no more than thirteen, with long straight yellow hair that blew very softly in the night breeze. She was very pale, almost white. Another shiver gripped Terence as the pale girl looked silently at Gawain.

"Hello G'winn," she said, almost too softly for Terence to hear.

With a sob, Gawain gasped, "Elaine!"

The most violent shiver of all wracked Terence's body. Elaine was Gawain's sister, who had died so many years before.

Elaine smiled slightly and beckoned to Gawain with one hand; then she turned and walked away. Gawain rose and stumbled behind as if in a trance.

"Go, Terence. Go after him," said a voice at his elbow. It was Robin, but a different Robin than Terence knew — a solemn, grave Robin whose lips curved in no smile and whose eyes held no mischief.

"Terence?" It was Lady Eileen, and her voice quavered with fear. "Who is that? Who is beside you?"

"Hurry, Terence, hurry," Robin whispered, and then he was gone.

"Terence?" Lady Eileen repeated, in a small voice.

"He's a friend, Eileen. I trust him," Terence managed to say. He stood and looked into the bushes into which Gawain had disappeared. "Come on, Eileen. We've got to go after Gawain." Terence took her firmly by the arm and pulled her to her feet. "He's in danger somehow. Come with me." She nodded, and Terence released her arm and led the way into the bushes.

The first thing he saw was one of Gawain's greaves, lying half concealed under a gorse bush. A few paces further was Gawain's shield. Terence realized suddenly that his own bow, arrows, sword, even his dagger were all back in the camp. He hesitated, but he knew he could not go back.

"Terence?" Eileen whispered. "What's going on? Why is he taking off his armor?"

"I don't know, Eileen. Hurry. We've got to catch up." They pushed on, following the trail of discarded armor, piece after piece thrown carelessly into the bushes, until Terence glimpsed a faint white light ahead of him and knew that they were near.

"Terence!" Eileen whispered fiercely. "Gawain's sword! There!"

Terence pushed roughly through a bush and saw

the Sword Galatine, stuck point downward into the gravel riverbank. Already halfway across the river, a boat glided toward the far shore, where an impossibly steep mountain rose up from the bank. In the prow of the boat stood the pale girl. Behind her sat Gawain. Eileen clutched Terence's arm.

"After them, Terence!" Robin's voice whispered hoarsely. Terence gulped, then grabbed Eileen's hand and stepped resolutely forward into the river. The water was frigid, but not deep, and they took another step. And then their feet were no longer in the water. From beneath the surface, a boat had risen, dripping, and was following in the invisible wake of Gawain's boat. Eileen's face was tight and filled with wonder, but she stared resolutely ahead at the approaching mountain. Terence hoped he looked that brave.

"There was no mountain there when we passed by earlier," Eileen whispered. "Where did it come from, Terence?"

"It's probably always been there. We're just seeing things differently tonight." Terence paused. "Have you ever heard of the Other World?" She shook her head. "There is another world, Eileen, one that exists alongside ours. It's the world of faeries, elves, gnomes, goblins, sprites, and such. I think that's where we're going."

"Have you been there before?"

Terence told Eileen briefly about his and Gawain's earlier visit to the Other World, about the kind and noble Ganscotter the Enchanter and his beautiful daughter Lorie. He told how Gawain had become the Maiden's Knight and had won Lorie's love. "But this time I don't think we'll find everything so pleasant," he concluded.

The boat crunched gently on the thin strip of gravel at the foot of the mountain, and Terence and Eileen scrambled ashore. The boat sank at once beneath the surface, and they looked at each other uneasily.

"How do we get back?" Eileen asked.

Terence hesitated, then said, "We'll find a way. In the stories, there's always some way."

"And you believe them?"

"With the Other World, what is there to believe but stories? Come on, Eileen. I guess we climb."

They climbed. The sides of the mountain were impossibly steep, but at every point they found another handhold. They no longer tried to follow Gawain and his pale guide; they had to follow the handholds, and there was never more than one, as if the mountain itself were guiding them. Soon they passed one of Gawain's shoes.

Terence climbed first and reached down often to help Eileen. They passed Gawain's other shoe, then the leather cuisses he wore on his legs under his armor, then his undercloak. All that Gawain had left was the thin linen shift he wore next to his skin. At last, near the top, they reached a grassy ledge and collapsed, trembling with exertion.

It was Eileen, her hands cut and bloody and her face streaked with grime, who stood first. "What is that?" she asked, pointing into a stand of pines.

It was a house, but smaller than any that Terence had ever seen. The top of the thatched roof was barely taller than Terence's head, and the door was no more than four feet high. "There are more over there!" Eileen said, pointing at a flash of white paint visible on the other side of a little stand of trees.

Taking Eileen's hand, Terence led the way through the trees until they stood at the end of a narrow street built into the side of the moun-tain, lined on both sides with miniature houses, neat little wooden structures with thatched roofs, high gables, and little flower boxes under every window.

"It's like a doll town," Eileen said wonderingly.

"Without the dolls," Terence added. The street was empty, and the houses were dark and forlorn-looking in the way that only deserted houses were. There was no feeling of suspended activity, no sense of expectancy, the way there was in a sleeping vil-lage. The houses were neat, cared for, clean, but empty. Terence and Eileen, still clutching each other's hands, walked slowly down the center of the street until it turned a corner and opened into a little level square. In the center of the square was Gawain, alone, leaning against a stone well.

"Good evening, Terence, Elai — Eileen," Gawain greeted them calmly. His white linen shift was soaked with sweat and smeared with blood. His hands were torn and dripping blood.

"Milord, let me see to your hands," Terence said, hurrying forward.

"Don't worry, lad. They'll be well in the morning."

Terence looked sharply into his master's face. Gawain's eyes were outlined with dark creases of exhaustion, and they looked mistily into the distance without focusing. "Milord," Terence said, examining Gawain's lacerations. "This is no dream."

At first Gawain did not move, but then he frowned and focused on his squire. "But I saw *her*. I see her only in my dreams."

"I saw her too, milord. It was your sister, wasn't it?" Gawain nodded dumbly. "We've made the crossing, milord. We're in the Other World."

"Terence!" Eileen shrieked. Both Terence and Gawain turned sharply and saw at the far side of the square a knight, fully armored and carrying a spiked mace that swung freely on its chain. The knight stepped resolutely toward them, and Gawain shoved Terence aside.

"See to Eileen, lad. Promise me you'll take care of her!"

"I vow it, milord."

The knight lifted his mace and swung it downward at Gawain, who jumped aside and threw himself into the knight's breastplate. The knight staggered backward a couple of steps, and Gawain fell, rolled, and stood up in a crouch. Then they did it all over again. Then again. Gawain would dodge the mace, try to land some sort of blow on the knight's armor, then scamper out of range. Everything that the mace hit crumbled or shattered. Gawain clearly was fighting through exhaustion, and a glancing blow from the mace had left blood welling from Gawain's right shoulder, but still he stayed on his feet.

At last he saw an opening. As the silent knight rushed forward, swinging his mace horizontally, at head level, Gawain slipped inside the swing and threw his whole weight against the knight's arm. The arm stopped abruptly in mid-swing, but the spiked ball on the chain continued its circuit with all the force of the knight's attack and buried itself in the knight's own helmet. A loud, inhuman squeal echoed through the deserted street, and the knight's arm tightened convulsively around Gawain. The two knights toppled together onto the flagstones and were still.

Terence and Eileen stared at the still forms. There was no sound, no movement. At last the knight's body stirred, and Gawain's voice came faintly from beneath the armor. "Terence, if it's not too much trouble—"

Together, Terence and Eileen were able to pull the dead knight off Gawain, and they removed the knight's helmet. Eileen moaned and looked away, and Terence took an involuntary step backwards. Under the visor was the head, snout, and curved tusks of a boar.

"So that's what that squeal was," Eileen said. "A dying pig."

At that moment, like a delayed echo, another squeal sounded from the edge of the wood. They whirled around. From the shadows under the trees glinted several pairs of eyes. There was a low grunting noise, and then a huge boar stepped into the moonlight, followed by others.

Gawain stooped and pulled the mace from the knight's limp gauntlet. Searching the body quickly, he found a small hand axe and tossed it to Terence. "Get Eileen back to the well," he commanded. They were just able to get their backs to the stone well at the center of the courtyard and to position Eileen between them before the boars charged.

For Terence, what followed was a dizzying whirl of instinctive reactions. He felt no pain or fear, made no plans, thought no thoughts, but simply existed in a stretch of clearheaded, tireless action that could have lasted for seconds or for hours. When it was over, he remembered battering boar after boar with his axe; he vaguely recalled seeing a tusk tear his right forearm and he remembered catching the tusk in his left hand and smashing the boar into the stones of the well; he remembered throwing himself into a charging boar and knocking it sprawling just before it could hit Eileen. But when the last boar had been killed or had fled, and Terence looked dazedly around the court, he could not account for the four carcasses that lay at his feet. A wave of dizziness rushed over him, and he leaned against the well for support.

"Good Gog, Terence," Gawain said from somewhere very far away. "If I don't have you knighted for this, I'll ... Good Gog, Terence!"

And then a softer voice, much closer, said, "Your arm, Terence. Hold it out and let me tie it up."

Weakly, Terence held out his right arm. "I guess they were angry that you killed the boar-knight, milord," he said.

"Sir Gawain, would you please dip some water from this well," said the soft voice. The voice sounded like Eileen's, except that it was gentle. "Sir Gawain? Oh, for heaven's sake, Gawain! I can't have you both fainting on me! Of all the inconsiderate.... Just like a man!"

"Yes," Terence thought. "It's Eileen, after all." And then he went to sleep.

VII

CHALLENGES IN THE NIGHT

Terence awoke to the smell of wildflowers and to a throbbing pain in his right arm. Opening his eyes, he found himself lying on a bundle of heather beside a stream. Nearby, Guingalet and the other horses cropped grass in a lush meadow. Gawain lay asleep nearby, but Eileen was awake, stitching the hem of her dress.

"What have you done to your dress?" Terence asked. His voice sounded weak and raspy.

Eileen glanced at him briefly, then resumed her sewing. "So you're awake, are you? How does your arm feel?"

Terence could not seem to focus his thoughts. "That dress barely covers your knees," he said. "Where's the rest of it?"

"Mostly wrapped around your arm and Gawain's shoulder. Some of it is on Gawain's feet. They got pretty chewed up climbing a mountain barefoot. Now answer me: How does your arm feel?"

"It hurts," Terence replied. "Where are we? How did we get here?"

"Well might you ask," Eileen said. "It took me hours to drag you and Gawain here. You sleep hard, Terence." Terence frowned, puzzled, and Eileen continued. "After the fight, when you and Gawain passed out, that village—You remember the little village?—just disappeared. There we were on the side of the mountain, with no food or water."

"So you dragged us up the mountain to this meadow?" Terence asked, frankly incredulous. "By yourself?"

Eileen hesitated. "No, a little man with a pointy beard helped me. Don't ask me who he was, because he wouldn't say."

"Never mind," Terence said. "I think I know. His name is Robin. He's the one I was talking to when you woke up last night, beside the river." Terence's head was clearing, and he noticed Gawain's armor arranged neatly under a tree. "I suppose Robin brought our horses and gear?"

Eileen nodded. "And food, and some ointment for your wounds." Terence closed his eyes again, unusually tired. Eileen spoke gently, "Before you go back to sleep, Terence, I want to thank you for saving my life from the boar last night."

Terence reddened and stammered, "Don't mention it, Lady Eileen."

"*Lady* Eileen, is it now?" she said briskly. "Are you angry with me, Squire Terence? You called me Eileen all night."

"I didn't!"

"You most certainly did, and since I have no desire to call you Squire Terence or Sir Terence or something witless like that, you may as well keep calling me Eileen. Now go to sleep."

Terence went to sleep. They ended up staying there by the brook for almost a month while Gawain and Terence recovered from their wounds. The food that Robin had given Eileen lasted a week, and by the end of that time Terence was able to prowl the woods and gather food. It was an idyllic time, spent telling stories and playing games. Neither the elfin village nor any wild boars ever reappeared. Terence and Eileen took long rides in the woods—Gawain complained that stirrups hurt his feet and refused to join them. Eileen told Terence about her life before she had gone to live with the Marquis of Alva, about her happy-go-lucky father and fiery Irish mother, who both died of a fever within a week of each other. Terence told Eileen of his childhood with the Hermit of the Gentle Wood and of his life and quests with Gawain. He told her about Tor and Plogrun, about Sir Kai and King Arthur, about Sir Lancelot and Guinevere.

Eileen was very interested in Guinevere. She listened to Terence's description, asked several questions, then pursed her lips and said, "Poor Sir Lancelot."

Terence stared. "Poor Sir Lancelot! What about the king?"

"Yes, of course, him too. They both love her. But from what you've said, it sounds as if King Arthur has figured her out. Sir Lancelot still has to learn."

"Learn what? What will he learn?"

"Just wait until Sir Lancelot is defeated by another knight and he's no longer the greatest knight in England. Then see what he finds out."

At last Gawain announced that they should be moving again. Both Terence and Eileen argued that Gawain's wounds needed more time to heal, but Gawain was firm. The next day found them riding down the gentle slopes of the far side of the mountain.

Two days later they met the first human they had seen since crossing to the Other World: a thin old man in a coarse hair shirt and hooded robe that hung over his face. Terence had seen enough religious pilgrims pass Camelot to recognize the traveler as one of these fervent souls. Gawain saluted the pilgrim and dismounted to walk beside him. The pilgrim returned Gawain's greeting pleasantly enough, but he neither slackened his pace nor gave the three riders more than a brief glance.

"Where are you bound, Father?" Gawain asked.

"Don't call me Father. I'm not a priest. I am a pilgrim, bound for holy places that will draw my mind to Christ Our Lord."

"Forgive me, sir, but are there any holy places here? I mean, we are in the Other World, are we not?"

"We are in what you would call so, child. And yes, there are holy places in every world. If holiness were confined to only one world, then no place would be holy."

Gawain frowned over this for a moment, then shrugged and asked, "Is one of the holy places you seek called the Green Chapel?"

The pilgrim stopped and looked at Gawain. Terence held his breath. "It is a holy place," the pilgrim said, "but I do not seek it. Do you?"

"I do. Can you direct me to it?"

"There is no need. In this world, to seek is to find." The pilgrim shook his head sadly and turned away from them. "The Green Chapel will find you."

They rode on, traveling single file, with Gawain in the lead and Terence in the rear. His job was to keep an eye on Eileen, which he did.

They made camp that night near a clear, ice-cold

river that ran off the mountain behind them. They had seen no one since they left the pilgrim, though Terence had often felt as if he were being watched. They ate a cold dinner and rolled up in their blankets to sleep off their long ride.

A few hours later, some noise wakened Terence. Beside him, Gawain was also awake. Gawain grinned and said, "Every blamed adventure we've had this quest has started this way, hasn't it? Waking up in the middle of the night."

Terence nodded to the still bundle that was Eileen. "Not everyone wakes up," he said.

They listened to the silent night for a few minutes, then Gawain said, "I'll stay up. You go on back to sleep."

At that moment a voice breathed from the darkness. "What are you?" Gawain and Terence leaped from their blankets, Gawain holding his sword, Terence his bow and an arrow. They saw nothing. "Why you're just a man," the voice said, with surprise. "Like me."

"Where are you, friend?" Gawain asked.

From a slight shadow on the plain, where Terence would not have thought a mouse could be concealed, a man stood and stepped closer. Gesturing at Gawain, he said, "When you rode down the mountain, this one was different. How have you changed your shiny skin, man?"

Terence did not understand the stranger, but Gawain said, "I am a knight, friend."

"A knight," the stranger whispered reflectively. "I want to become a knight. A knight is a god?"

"No, friend. I am only a man. Look here." Gawain pointed at his armor. "It is not skin; it is a knight's armor. Clothes of metal."

The stranger reached out a hand and, at arm's length, touched one of the metal gauntlets. "You wear this?"

"I do."

"I want to become a knight. What is a knight?"

Gawain smiled and said, "A knight is a fighter, one who protects the weak from those who are stronger than they."

"I can fight," the stranger said with calm simplicity.

"Can you?" Gawain said politely.

"I will show you," the stranger said, and without another word threw himself at Gawain. Terence saw Gawain's sword lift, then stop, and then both men went over with a clatter onto the armor. They rolled together for a moment, then Gawain threw the stranger from him. The man rolled neatly to his feet and whirled to face Gawain, smiling happily. "You *do* fight," he said, with clear pleasure.

"I do," Gawain said. He drove his sword into the

ground. "Come on, then, friend."

The stranger feinted to his left, then whirled with uncanny speed to his right and grabbed Gawain's arm and leg. Terence watched with amazement as Gawain rose into the air, then crashed into the dirt, the stranger still gripping him. Gawain countered with an out-thrust leg, but the stranger only gripped the leg and threw Gawain backwards again. Gawain stood quickly and wiped his brow. "You *do* fight, too," he said. The stranger smiled brightly and attacked again.

"Hey!" Gawain exclaimed. "Stop that!"

The stranger backed away. "Stop what?"

"Clawing like that!"

"Why?"

"It's not knightly."

"Not what?"

"When knights fight, they don't scratch."

"Why not?"

Gawain considered this for a minute, then said, "Because we are men, not beasts."

The stranger straightened out of his wrestler's crouch and said, "Can a knight not even scratch when he fights a beast?"

Gawain hesitated. "What sort of beasts do you fight?"

"Lions. Bears. Wolves. Dogs. Serpents."

"If a knight fights a lion bare-handed, he may claw," Gawain conceded. "But not when he fights a man. And no biting, either," he added hastily.

The stranger nodded slowly. "I want to be a knight," he muttered.

The two men wrestled for almost an hour, and though Gawain threw the stranger often and always seemed to escape the stranger's grip, Terence could see that Gawain was fighting a defensive battle. The stranger was stronger and a better wrestler. Only the stranger's meticulous care not to use his nails or teeth kept Gawain in the contest at all. Several times the stranger would dive into an opening, then check his attack abruptly, clench his fists, and mutter "No scratching." Then Gawain would throw him. Terence shook his head with wonder and kept an arrow notched. If Gawain got into danger, he would shoot the stranger without hesitation.

He glanced at Eileen's blankets, still motionless, and frowned. Surely she was not still asleep. Watching the contest from the corner of his eye he crossed to Eileen's pallet and said, "Eileen?" Nothing moved. He knelt swiftly and pulled the blanket back. Only a leather bag and a few rumpled clothes lay there: Eileen was gone. "Milord! Milord!" he shouted.

"Terence," Gawain gasped, "I'm not really free just now."

"Milord, Eileen's gone."

Gawain broke away from the fight and, keeping his eyes on the stranger, repeated, "Gone?"

"Not here," Terence explained.

Gawain straightened. "Friend, I should like to fight longer, but I must stop now," he said.

The stranger smiled brightly and nodded. "Very well. It was a good fight."

"Unless," Gawain said slowly, "you are the one who took our friend, the Lady Eileen."

"The lady who was with you earlier? No, she was gone when I arrived. Did you not know it?" Gawain shook his head. "Then it must be Hag Annis," the stranger said.

"What is Hag Annis?"

"She's a witch, the bad kind, you know. She eats all sorts of vile things, but her favorite food is young maidens."

Terence felt faint and could not speak. "Where does this Hag Annis live?" Gawain demanded.

"Down the river, not far. Why?"

"So we can go save our friend, of course. A knight always..." This was the last that Terence heard until a moment later Gawain called, "Terence! Get the horses!" but it was too late then. Terence was already a quarter of a mile away, running along the riverbank.

Hag Annis's cottage was only about two miles

away, and Terence was there in just over ten minutes, even carrying the bow and one arrow that he had been holding when he left. It was a tiny hovel with a roof of bound twigs. Just outside the door, a bent old woman stooped over a huge pile of logs and worked busily with a tinderbox. Behind her was a thick wooden post, and Eileen was seated at its base, her hands behind her. The woman cackled something, and Eileen replied angrily. Terence sank to the ground, weak with relief. She was alive.

Terence crept closer. The hag's skin was a dark, mottled blue, and she wore a cloak of shimmery black material that seemed to be alive itself, dancing and grimacing. The hag struck a spark and leaped away from the pile of tinder. It caught, and slowly a flame began to grow. Terence crawled slowly forward. He was in range now for a good bowshot, but as he had only one arrow he wanted to make it absolutely certain.

"Now, my pretty little thing," the hag said, cackling, "I like to give a maiden a choice. Would you rather be roasted whole or sliced and fried?"

"I think I'd rather be poisoned," Eileen snapped. "Then we could both die."

"Oh dear, no." The hag giggled. "I can't be done in like that. No poison ever found that I can't eat. But they all taste so nasty—except some toadstools. You wouldn't want to taste nasty, now."

"I do so. And furthermore, I hope I disagree with you."

"No worry, no worry. I've a wonderful digestion, though now you mention it, I can't abide eggs. You haven't been eating eggs recently have you?"

"I love eggs," Eileen replied promptly. "I ate seven of them for dinner."

"Hee-hee, it's almost a pity to kill you, you're so much fun."

"Well, I think so too," Eileen said. "Shall we let me go, then?"

The hag looked mournful. "Then what would poor Annis eat for dinner?"

"How about some nice toadstools?"

"Hee-hee, you really are delightful," the hag declared, cackling louder. She poked tentatively at the fire with a long, sharpened stick.

"Look here, Annis," Eileen said. "You know you won't live until morning anyway, why should you kill me?"

"Why won't I live till morning, hey?"

"Because the two great knights I rode with will have your heart out as soon as they find out that you've done me in."

Terence notched his arrow and took careful aim at Annis's left eye, but a spark jumped out of the fire, and the hag skipped hastily away from it. "Don't set your hopes too high, my little dear," she said. "I've a spell cast on me that protects me. I can never be killed by a man, though enough of the beasts have tried. They only make me stronger. Vermin, they are, and not worth my notice."

Terence hesitated. If the hag were speaking the truth and he could not kill her, then to shoot her would only announce his presence.

"You don't like men, I take it," Eileen said. Terence guessed that she was trying to keep the hag occupied with conversation.

"We'd all be better off without them, with just women. Lecherous goats they are, all of them. In fact, I sometimes turn them into goats."

Terence crept around the periphery of the firelight until he was behind Eileen.

Eileen snorted. "All this talk about your spells and your powers, and I haven't seen a bit of it. It took you twenty minutes just to light a fire."

"Ah but dear, a good cookfire has to be just right. Otherwise part of you won't get done and another part will be just burned up."

Eileen swallowed, but in a moment she continued bravely. "Look here, Annis. If you're so fond of women, why do you eat them? Why don't you eat men, if you hate them so much?"

Annis made a rude noise and said, "Disgusting. That's why."

Terence was directly behind Eileen now, and he

saw the outline of Eileen's arms, tied behind the post. In the shadow of the fire, Terence could almost make out the outline of her hands. Right between them was where she would be tied. If he shot an arrow at that spot, it would cut her bonds, and she could escape.

His arrow went true. He heard a dull thud and saw Eileen jump. The hag looked around suspiciously, but Terence had dropped to the dirt. After a moment, she shrugged and went back to poking at the fire with her long, pointed stick. Eileen twisted and tugged until, suddenly, her hands pulled free. Immediately she tucked them behind her again. The hag stepped away from the fire and looked at it for a long moment, then nodded.

"All right, dear. You'll have to stand up now. This is the difficult bit, and I hope you won't be too noisy. I have to run a skewer through you, to hold you steady while you roast." She produced a long, wicked-looking metal skewer. "Now stand up, dear." Eileen stood, still holding her arms behind the post. The hag stepped close, beaming, and said, "Now this might sting a bit, love."

Eileen did not answer. As Annis bent, Eileen whipped her arms from behind the post and shoved the hag roughly backwards. "Into the fire with you!" she cried. The hag's old eyes flew wide open, and she shrieked awfully. Eileen stooped and picked up the metal skewer that Annis had dropped. Terence leaped forward, but there was nothing left to do. The hag, who had fallen backward into the fire, roared out a very masculine bellow and then exploded into a searing white flame, too bright to look at. When the light was gone, Terence stepped up beside Eileen. All that was left of Hag Annis was her shiny black cloak.

"No wonder she was afraid of fire," Eileen said.

"Are you hurt?" Terence asked.

"No, but no thanks to you," she snapped, wheeling to face him. "What sort of imbecilic notion was that? Cutting my bonds with an arrow! What if you had missed?"

Terence sniffed loftily. "Never occurred to me."

"Idiot! Moron! Domnoddy! Leatherskulled block!"

Terence glared at her with growing anger. He started to retort but at the last second saw how brightly the fire glinted in Eileen's eyes and realized she was crying. He made a hesitant move toward her, then stopped.

"Well?" she sobbed. "Are you just going to stand there?" Terence pulled her to his chest, and held her tightly. "Domnoddy," she said in a muffled voice.

"Huh. Better off being eaten, I'd say," came Gawain's voice. Terence and Eileen parted quickly. At the edge of the firelight, Gawain sat on Guingalet.

"She's all right, milord," Terence said, trying to sound gruff and businesslike.

"You're certainly in a better position to know that than I am," Gawain said solemnly. "Is the hag here?"

"Eileen killed her," Terence said.

Eileen looked surprised. "How did you know about the hag? And how did you find me, Terence?"

Gawain answered for them both. "We met a man back in camp who told us about her."

"A man?"

"Well, yes," Gawain said with a smile. "But I believe he wants to be a knight."

Months passed. The weather turned warm, then hot, and still they found no Green Chapel. They fought bears, lions, and once a dragon. They saw dogs with the faces of ugly, grumpy men and the feet of ducks and witnessed a fierce battle between tiny men, no more than six inches high, and a flock of white cranes. Gawain killed a slime-coated serpent that crawled from a swamp, and Terence shot half a quiver of arrows into a giant screeching bird, which flew away in search of less troublesome prey. But these moments of excitement were rare: most days they simply rode all day, then made camp and prepared to do the same the next.

The heat lessened during the days, and the nights

grew cool. The evenings came sooner, leaves changed color and fell, frost appeared in the mornings, and ivy bloomed along the hedgerows. Their clothes were threadbare and often mended, and Gawain's armor was dull and covered with tiny hammer marks where Terence had pounded out larger dents. Gawain and Terence still sparred with swords most evenings. Gawain wished that they could make some lances and practice tilting, but Terence was able to convince him that lances would only be in the way on their long rides. Terence had never liked tilting, and his ignominious defeat at King Arthur's hands in his one actual joust (of which he had never informed Gawain) had not made it any more attractive.

The morning frosts grew thicker, and the skies hung low, weighed down with a winter of snow. They were all weary of traveling, but Terence wished they could wander forever. The approach of winter brought the New Year, and Gawain's part of the Green Knight's bargain grew nearer. Terence could tell from the stars that the winter solstice was near. New Year's Eve, Gawain's appointed time, would soon follow.

Then one day they rode out of a thick evergreen forest onto a rolling dale that stretched before the most delicately constructed, most inviting castle Terence had ever seen. The turrets tapered to perfect

points as they rose impossibly high into the air —
the top of the central keep was actually hidden in
a low cloud — and gay banners festooned every
window. There was no moat, and the gate was open
and unguarded.

"What a beautiful castle!" Eileen exclaimed.

Two riders trotted out of the castle gate and
stopped, staring at the three ragged travelers, then
rode near. It was a man and a woman, and both
hailed the three cheerily.

"Welcome, travelers," the man said. "You wear
the weariness of many miles in your faces."

"And many months, sir," Gawain said.

"Then I perceive you are on quest." The man
smiled. "How may I help?"

"First," Gawain said, "perhaps you could tell us
what day is today."

"Why, do you not know?" the lady trilled mirth-
fully. "Indeed, you have been questing long. Today
is Christmas Eve."

Gawain raised his eyes to the skies and murmured
something that Terence could not hear, then — to
Terence's astonishment — quietly crossed himself,
the way that the continental priests at Camelot used
to do.

"Perhaps I can help you find what you seek," the
man said.

"Indeed, I hope so, for I have little time," Gawain replied. "I seek the Green Chapel and the knight who is lord there."

The man smiled widely and exclaimed, "Then seek no further, O knight. The Green Chapel lies not two miles from here."

VIII

BERCILAK'S KEEP

Terence's heart sank. For nine months they had ridden without direction, never knowing whether they were near or far from the Green Chapel, but as the time drew near they had come smash up to it. Eileen closed her eyes and sighed softly. Even Gawain looked taken back. The woman spoke. "I pray you all to stay and celebrate this holy Christmas feast with us, if it be possible."

Gawain looked at Eileen and Terence, then nodded. "I must go to the Green Chapel in one week's time, on New Year's Eve, but until then, we are pleased to accept your hospitality, my lady."

The lord and lady of the castle led them into the courtyard, where a regiment of servants appeared. Grooms saw to their horses, a chattering gaggle of tirewomen swept Eileen through one door, and a bowing steward and several obsequious pages conducted Gawain and Terence through another to a gorgeously furnished chamber. The steward bowed deeply before Gawain and said, "If you have no objection, perhaps you could stay in this room, sir? This doorway across from the bed leads to a bedchamber for your squire." He cleared his throat and looked slightly pained. "Now, if I might venture one more convenience, perhaps you would accept some new clothes. You have traveled far, and some...er...fresh garments might be more comfortable." Gawain nodded solemnly, and the steward paced majestically from the room.

Gawain chuckled. "What he meant was that our clothes look like a gravedigger's castoffs."

An hour later, Gawain and Terence had washed and were elegantly dressed. Terence began arranging Gawain's armor and said, "Maybe I'll have a chance to do some real repair on this armor while we're here."

"Why?" Gawain asked. Terence glanced at him doubtfully, then understood: Gawain would face only one more adversary in this life—the Green Knight—and that one he would face without a struggle. Terence turned away, blinking back sudden tears. "Shall we go find Eileen?" Gawain asked.

Eileen was in a comfortable sitting room chatting

politely with their host and hostess. She too had been well treated: she wore a rich blue gown over an underdress of the palest blue silk. Firelight glimmered in her hair, and Terence wondered with amazement whatever had happened to her freckles. They were gone, and she did not look at all like a child.

"Come in, come in," their host called heartily. "Warm yourselves!" Gawain sat, and Terence stood behind his master's chair.

"No, Terence," Gawain said. "Not this time. Sit beside me." Gawain pulled him irresistibly into a chair between him and Eileen. "I have not been so comfortable in almost a year," he said to the lord and lady.

"If that is so, then we are content," their host said. "I am called Sir Bercilak, and this is my wife, the Lady Marion. Our home and our bounty is yours so long as you desire."

"I shall be glad to spend this week with you. I am Sir Gawain, this is the Lady Eileen, and this is my squire Terence."

Sir Bercilak beamed, and Lady Marion said, "We could ask no greater happiness than to entertain the Maiden's Knight. And is this indeed the fearless Terence who is praised so highly in this world? We are honored."

Terence reddened and peeked at Eileen. Gawain

said, "It is he, and he is well-deserving of whatever praise he is given. Nor could there be a more courageous questing lady than the Lady Eileen."

Sir Bercilak laughed loudly, as if Gawain had told a joke, and declared. "We shall hear your tale at our feast! Indeed, you shall be merry with us for this week before you go on your way."

On the first two nights of the Christmas feast, they were entertained by a wandering minstrel, who told a long and magical tale of the legendary hero Cucholinn. On the third night, at Sir Bercilak's request, Gawain told the story of their adventures. He told it from the beginning, but omitted any reference to the beheading, so that Sir Bercilak and Lady Marion might think he was meeting the Green Knight for a friendly joust. Gawain could not match the rhythmic cadences of the minstrel, but he told his story in the best courtly style, making humdrum events sound exciting and making other events, like Terence's part in the fight with the boars, seem almost superhuman. When he was done, Sir Bercilak began jovially retelling to no one in particular the parts of the tale he had liked best, and Lady Marion, ignoring her husband, proclaimed the story marvelously told.

"Now, how will we amuse ourselves the rest of the week?" Sir Bercilak said. "Sir Gawain, have you a fancy to go a-hunting with me tomorrow?"

Gawain shook his head apologetically. "I thank you, Sir Bercilak, but I feel I have been hunting for too long."

"For shame, husband!" Lady Marion said gently, "that having heard of Sir Gawain's great travels you would now allow him no rest! Sir Gawain has no wish to rise with you at dawn for the chase; he shall lie abed as long as he wishes tomorrow."

Gawain smiled and said, "Indeed, I had feared that my slothfulness since I have been with you would be noticed. In sooth, my bed has been all too comfortable."

"You shall stay there as long as you wish!" Sir Bercilak declared. "And when you arise, you shall hunt here in the castle for whatever diversion you like. Say! I have an idea!" He paused, as if expecting to be congratulated, then said, "Sir Gawain, agree to this: whatever I capture during the day, I shall give to you at evening, and whatever you capture you shall give to me."

"I fear you shall find yourself empty-handed at the end of the day," Gawain protested, smiling.

"No no, I've always had good luck hunting!" Sir Bercilak said earnestly.

"My lord," Lady Marion said, "I think Sir Gawain meant that he would have captured nothing to give to you."

"Oh, I don't fear that! Come, Sir Gawain, is it agreed?"

"Very well—agreed," Gawain said.

The next morning, Terence rose shortly after dawn and looked out his window onto the gentle hills below. In the distance he saw a band of horsemen and very faintly heard the yelping of greyhounds. Sir Bercilak was already hard at the chase. He opened the door to Gawain's room a crack and peeked in. Gawain was still sound asleep. Terence dressed himself in a fine embroidered outfit and surveyed the generous breakfast that the castle servants had laid out for him.

There was a light tapping on the door, and Eileen peeked in. She wore a long dress of pale yellow that just matched her hair. Terence beckoned her in and, with a vague sense of surprise, realized that he loved her. He nodded toward the tray and asked, "Would you like some breakfast?"

"No, thank you. I've just finished my own," she said. They stood for a moment looking at each other. Then Eileen said, "You look nice this morning."

"*I* look nice?" Terence gasped. "*You* look... nice, too."

The corner of Eileen's mouth quivered. "Well, I did think I looked fine this morning, but of course all you could talk about was breakfast."

Terence grinned, feeling the awkwardness dissolve,

and said, "Oh, now I understand. You don't think I look nice at all; you just said so to force me to compliment you. Vanity of vanities...."

Eileen stuck her tongue out at him and crossed the room to the window. "Well, I will at least admit that you look *cleaner* than I'm used to seeing you," she said in her grandest manner.

"What about you? I'd forgotten what color your hair was until the other day when you first washed our journey out of it."

For some reason, this seemed sad, and they were silent for a minute, looking together out the window. At last Terence said, "What do you think you'll do now that...now that the quest is over?"

She shrugged slightly and said, "I don't know. What about you? I guess you'll go off to become a knight, won't you?"

"I don't know. That's Gawain's plan for me, but once he's..." Terence felt a lump rise in his throat, and his eyes filled. "Well, being a knight was never as exciting to me as to him." Terence blinked, and a tear rolled halfway down his cheek and hung there. Wordlessly, Eileen lifted a strand of her hair and gently wiped it away. Terence could feel the softness of her hair on his cheek for several seconds afterward.

"What will you do then?" she asked.

"First, I'll see to you. I mean, I'll take you wherever you want."

She colored slightly and said, "But I don't know where that is."

"I'll take you to Camelot, then."

Eileen smiled doubtfully, but nodded. They both realized that neither of them knew the way to Camelot anyway. Eileen rested her head very softly against Terence's shoulder and said, "Thank you."

A faint murmur of voices came to their ears, and they both jumped and stepped apart. The door to Gawain's room was slightly open, and from within came a woman's soft laughter. Terence and Eileen looked at each other, then tiptoed to the door and peeked in. Lady Marion, in a silken nightdress, sat at the foot of Gawain's bed. Gawain held his blankets tightly across his chest. From Gawain's gestures Terence guessed that Gawain was suggesting that she wait for him in another room. Lady Marion laughed again and settled herself more comfortably at the foot of Gawain's bed. Terence and Eileen stepped away from the door and looked at each other with consternation.

"That's not decent!" Terence whispered.

"To say the least," Eileen agreed.

"Should we walk in and rescue him?" Terence asked.

Eileen frowned, then shook her head. "But that might embarrass Lady Marion. Shouldn't we let Gawain take care of it himself?"

They discussed it for several more minutes, but in the end decided to do nothing. For the next hour, they sat in Terence's room and speculated in whispers on Lady Marion's motives. Every few minutes one would peek into Gawain's room and then return to tell the other that matters were the same.

The murmur of voices from the next room stopped, and a moment later a door shut. Gawain called, "All right, Terence. You can come in." Terence and Eileen hurried into Gawain's chamber. Gawain glanced quizzically at Eileen and said, "Why Terence, I didn't know you had a woman in your room, too."

"At least mine is dressed," Terence replied.

"Tough luck."

Terence reddened, and Eileen said coolly, "Perhaps I had best wait in the sitting room until your conversation is ready for company, Gawain."

Gawain grinned appreciatively and bowed to her. With great dignity, Eileen left the room, and Gawain said, "You've a fine lady there, Terence."

Terence blushed again and said, "What happened, milord?"

Gawain stopped grinning and frowned. "Just what it looked like. The only way I could finally get rid of her was to let her give me one kiss."

"Maybe she got the message, though," Terence suggested.

"Nay, lad. As she left, she said Sir Bercilak would go out hunting again tomorrow, and the way she said it... well, you understand."

Terence nodded. "So what should you do?"

"I don't know," Gawain said, his brow furrowed. "As Sir Bercilak's guest I can't... well, I couldn't do anything to break faith with my host, even if I wanted to. To do so would be —"

"Like Sir Lancelot?"

Terence had allowed disapproval to creep into his voice, and Gawain glanced quickly at him. "Ay, lad. But Lady Marion's no Guinevere. She's witty and bright — brighter than her husband, at any rate — and I've no wish to ruin her credit with her lord by bearing tales."

"If you don't do something, she'll be back tomorrow."

"Let her come then," Gawain said with sudden decision. "We'll just see to it that nothing happens. Tomorrow, do what you did today. Wait in your room with the door open. I'll call if I need you to walk in and interrupt."

Sir Bercilak returned that evening with almost a dozen deer, all of them true hunter's trophies. According to the terms of their bargain, Sir Bercilak stood in the castle court amid the pile of carcasses and grandly presented them to Gawain with his compliments. "Now," he said jovially, "what have you achieved this day to present to me?"

"Most of what I captured today, I am loth to give you, as it is already yours. Thus I do not offer you a fine luncheon and much good wine," Gawain said. "But one thing I surely won today." Before Terence knew what was happening, Gawain stepped forward and kissed Sir Bercilak soundly on the lips.

Sir Bercilak roared with laughter. "Faith, you've had a better day than I! I'd give much to learn where you captured that!"

"Nay, that was no part of our bargain," Gawain said. Sir Bercilak laughed loudly again. Lady Marion, watching from a doorway, smiled.

The next morning Sir Bercilak went hunting again, carrying a thick boar spear. Terence awoke early and dressed, then from his window pensively watched Sir Bercilak's party ride away. A servant brought in his breakfast tray and looked surprised to see him awake. A light tap came from the door, and Terence leaped across the room to open it. As he had hoped, it was Eileen, beautiful in a long gown of green silk with gold embroidery.

She smiled. "Do you still want to share your breakfast with me?"

He grinned. "Come along."

She stepped to the center of the room and stopped. Then, with the resigned air of one who is prompting an imbecile, she said, "You look nice today, Terence."

"Thank you," Terence replied. She waited, but he only grinned.

"Domnoddy," Eileen said, chuckling. "All right, I'll say it. Do I look nice today?"

"No, not nice. You're beautiful, Eileen."

Eileen stood motionless. At last she said breathlessly, "That's not playing fair, Terence."

Terence nodded. "Sorry. How about a slice of ham?"

For a moment they busied themselves with breakfast, then Eileen said, "I tried to talk to you alone all evening. What was that all about in the courtyard yesterday?" Terence looked puzzled, and she explained. "The kiss! Who did Gawain get that kiss from? Lady Marion?"

"Yes." Terence told her about the kiss, about Gawain's expectation that Lady Marion would return, and then explained Gawain's plan.

"So you're stuck here until Gawain gets out of bed?" she asked. Terence nodded. "Want some company?" He nodded again, more vigorously. "All right, I'll send your steward," she said, standing. Terence gaped, and Eileen collapsed onto the bed, smothering a fit of giggles. "Of course I'll stay with you."

"It's not that," Terence said, trying to recover his dignity. "It's just that I'm terrified of that toplofty steward."

Just then they heard the thud of a door shutting firmly and the trill of a woman's laugh. Terence and Eileen froze, then simply continued their conversation in lowered voices. They talked for over an hour, about a thousand things, and all the while from Gawain's room came the murmur of light-hearted dalliance. When the conversation next door stopped, they were silent as well. Then Gawain called, "All right, Terence. She's gone."

Terence pulled open the door and stood on the threshold. "Um...did you have a nice morning, milord?"

"Pleasant enough," Gawain smiled. "And you?"

"Oh, yes."

Gawain nodded hello to Eileen and said, "I assume Terence has told you about our arrangement?" She nodded. "Well, it went today much as it went yesterday," he said.

"A kiss?" Terence asked bluntly. Gawain nodded. "Do you think she's given up this time?"

Gawain shook his head. "Sir Bercilak hunts fox tomorrow. How about a ride this afternoon?"

So the three of them rode all afternoon along the dales, arriving back at the castle only minutes before Sir Bercilak returned. He triumphantly presented Gawain a huge black boar. There, in the growing shadow of the central keep, he and Gawain exchanged trophies again: a boar for a kiss. As he had the day before, Sir Bercilak treated the kiss as a huge joke and good-naturedly tried to guess from which of the servant girls Gawain was capturing his prizes. Terence and Eileen exchanged expressive looks, and Lady Marion laughed merrily.

And so it was that Terence and Eileen met again the next morning to wait outside Gawain's chamber. The curious behavior of Lady Marion had distracted Terence for the past two days, but this morning he had awakened with the painful realization that tomorrow Gawain would go to the Green Chapel to die. He was quiet, and Eileen allowed him his private thoughts. Only once did she speak: "Can you tell me what you're thinking, Terence?"

He looked at her gravely, started to shake his head, then said quietly, "I love you, Eileen."

"I know," she said calmly. "I love you, too."

Terence promptly burst into tears. Eileen walked to him, buried her face in the hollow of his shoulder, and let him stroke her hair while he wept. They stood that way for several minutes, until Terence pushed her to his arm's length, looked into her eyes, and said, "At least I'll still have you."

"Always," she said and led him to a chair. She sat at his feet, silently watching his face. They were still there half an hour later when Gawain walked abruptly into the room, a bemused expression on his face. From his hand dangled a shining green sash.

Terence stood, looking intently at his master's face. "Is she gone?" he asked.

"Just one kiss, like before," Gawain said.

"What do you have there, Gawain?" Eileen asked, indicating the green sash.

"A girdle she gave me before she left," Gawain said. He held it up and studied it. "She says that so long as I wear this girdle, I can never be killed, by any hand whatsoever."

It took Terence a second to grasp the full significance of this. "Then you're saved! Wear the girdle to the Green Chapel and let the cursed knight do his worst!"

Eileen sank to her knees and breathed a prayer of thanksgiving while Terence repeated "You're saved!" with greater and greater animation. He lifted Eileen to her feet and hugged her joyously.

"You're forgetting something," Gawain interrupted.

"What?" Terence demanded.

"My bargain with Sir Bercilak."

"Gawain," Eileen said, "you're not thinking of giving up this belt now that you have it are you?"

"That was the bargain."

"Milord, it's just a stupid game! You won't give up your life just to be true to that dimwit Sir Bercilak!" Terence could not believe his ears.

"Do not forget that he's our host, Terence," Gawain said reprovingly.

"All right, that dimwit our host. Answer my question!"

"Well, I'll admit that it does seem somewhat disproportionate." Gawain nodded. "It's hard to believe that Sir Bercilak would really ask me to give up my last chance. Perhaps I could give it to him, then ask for it back."

"Don't be stupid, milord!" Terence snapped. "What if he knows this girdle? Do you think he'll return it once he knows his wife has been calling on you every morning in her invisible nightdress?"

"I see your point," Gawain agreed reluctantly. "I hate to break my word to him, though."

Eileen asked reasonably, "Which do you hate more: breaking your word or dying?"

"I don't know. I've never done either."

෴

He had to choose one or the other, though, and in the end he chose to break his word. When Sir Bercilak returned from the hunt, proudly wielding the aromatic pelt of a large red fox, Gawain dutifully gave him a kiss but kept the magic girdle. Terence sighed with relief and spent the rest of the evening in a daze of blissful contentment. That night, the burden of a year lifted, he slept soundly and peacefully, dreaming of Eileen.

IX

THE GREEN CHAPEL

The next day, Terence awoke long after sunrise, well rested and pleasantly aware of an overwhelming sense of well-being. After a moment he remembered why: Gawain would survive his meeting with the Green Knight, and Eileen loved him. He could imagine no greater happiness. He rolled out of bed and strolled into Gawain's room. Gawain was already up and was trying to lace on his armor.

"Hallo, slug-a-bed," Gawain called. "If it's not too much bother, perhaps your worship would give me a bit of assistance here."

Terence chuckled and began untying the loose knots that Gawain had tied. "I'll start by doing these right, if it's all the same with you."

"Oh, ay. Do as you please. Don't want to inconvenience you, after all." Terence grinned absently and swiftly knotted a few laces. Gawain examined his battered armor and said, "I wish I'd let you work on this when you suggested it. I may need it today after all."

"Whatever for?" Terence asked.

"It's hard to tell how the Green Knight will take it, finding that he can't kill me. He didn't seem especially good-natured to me."

Terence left his lacing for a moment and frowned. "You mean you may have to fight him?" He recalled unhappily the Green Knight's monstrous frame.

"Now don't take on like that," Gawain said. "Believe me, the chance to fight is like a gift of God compared to what I was expecting."

That was true, Terence admitted, but as he finished fastening Gawain's armor he felt a twinge of uneasiness that marred his perfect happiness. He was able to put his anxiety aside when they stepped into the sitting room, however, because Eileen was there. He and Eileen smiled a tender welcome to each other. Gawain noted their smiles with obvious amusement, but Terence did not care.

Sir Bercilak bustled into the room, a broad smile lighting his face. "Sir Gawain! I have wonderful news for you!"

"Have you?" Gawain answered.

"I do indeed. When you first arrived, while you were still out on the east hill, I noticed you crossed yourself, and I said to myself, 'Bercilak, now there's a good Christian knight.'"

"Oh no," Gawain disclaimed politely.

"Yes, I did. I fancy few things go on around me that I don't notice." Terence met Eileen's quick, expressive glance. Gawain only bowed slightly. "So," Sir Bercilak continued, "I've been puzzling ever since you arrived how I was going to provide a mass for you to hear before going out, because I know that good Christian knights all hear mass before going questing. You see," he added apologetically, "I don't really have what you'd call a priest here all the time."

"I thank you for the thought," Gawain said. "But I shall contrive to go on quest without hearing a mass this time." Terence chuckled inwardly at the relief in Gawain's voice.

"Ah, but wait till you hear my news," Sir Bercilak beamed. "Last night, after we had all gone to bed, who do you think came to my gates? A priest! That's who! What do you think of that?"

"How delightful," Gawain said.

"Well, it's not quite all that you could hope. He says he's on a journey of penance himself, and he won't serve the mass."

"What a pity." Gawain sighed.

"But he says he'd be happy to hear your confession! What do you think of that?"

"My confession?" Gawain repeated blankly.

"It's a stroke of good fortune if ever I've heard one," Sir Bercilak continued blithely. "I know how real Christian knights like you like to have themselves all confessed up before going into battle. You wouldn't believe the time I had convincing this priest to hear your confession—him wanting to keep to himself—but I don't grudge the effort."

"How can I say thank you?" Gawain said, shaking his head.

Sir Bercilak chortled happily and said, "No need, no need. Happy to do it. But you'd best hurry. He's waiting for you outside right now."

Sir Bercilak bustled out, and Gawain gazed wonderingly after him. "You were right, Terence. Dimwit."

They filed downstairs to the courtyard, where Guingalet and Terence's horse were already saddled. Sir Bercilak had disappeared, but they had no trouble finding the priest. He sat on a shady bench by the stables, dressed in a monk's black robe and cowl. Gawain looked at him resignedly then said, "Wait here, Terence. I suppose I had better go talk to this priest—Bercilak having gone to so much trouble."

Gawain walked over to the priest and sat beside him on the bench. For a minute Terence watched; then Gawain gestured to Terence. Puzzled, Terence crossed the busy yard to where they sat.

"Here he is," Gawain said to the priest. The priest nodded and smiled at Terence. The top half of his face was shaded darkly by the cowl, but his smile was pleasant. Terence bowed.

"Have you confidence in him?" the priest asked Gawain.

"I would trust Terence with my life," Gawain said.

"I do not mean confidence in his ability," the priest said. "Have you confidence in his fitness?"

"Fitness for what?"

"Fitness to go to the Green Chapel. There is no blemish that can be hidden in that place. To take an unworthy escort there is as foolish as to go there unworthy oneself."

"I know no one so worthy as Terence—in any way."

The priest looked again at Terence, nodded, then turned back to Gawain. "And yourself?"

"Am I worthy?" Gawain asked. The priest nodded. "I fear I am not," Gawain said.

"Do you speak sincerely? Or do you say that only because you believe a knight should always show modesty?"

Gawain glanced at the priest sharply. He started to speak, then frowned and said, "In truth, you may be right. I may have spoken purely out of habit."

"Modesty is not a bad habit, after all," the priest

commented. "Although humility would be better. So, what have you to confess besides secret pride?"

Gawain stared wordlessly at the priest. Terence wished he could leave, but found himself unable to interrupt to excuse himself. "It seems that my secret pride is not secret from you. Can you see right into my heart, I wonder?" Gawain asked.

"I see no more than any man could see if he chose," the priest said. "Again, what else have you to confess?"

"I . . . I have not been a good Christian, Father."

The priest snorted derisively. "And what the hell is that, I'd like to know?" Gawain's mouth opened again, and he blinked several times. "Well," pursued the priest, "what do you mean 'good Christian'?"

"One who . . . who lives a moral life, I suppose."

"Don't be an ass," the priest said. "If that's all you have to say, you're wasting my time."

"I'm sorry, Father," Gawain said. "I'm afraid that I don't know how to confess."

"Then you must learn to be ashamed."

"Ashamed of what?"

"Find out," the priest said decisively. He stood abruptly and walked out of the courtyard and through the open gate. Gawain watched, frowning, until he was completely out of sight.

Ten minutes later, having received directions to

the Green Chapel, Terence and Gawain took their leave of Eileen and Lady Marion. Under his breath, he whispered to Eileen, "We'll be back."

"I'll be waiting," she replied. Gawain thanked Lady Marion for her hospitality, charged her with his thanks to Sir Bercilak, then led the way out of the gate toward the Green Chapel.

"You have that magic girdle, milord?" Terence asked after a minute.

"Did you think I would forget it? It's beneath my armor."

There seemed nothing more to say, and they rode in silence for several more minutes. Terence could not escape a growing uneasiness. They rode through a small stand of trees that grew along a brook, then stopped. Before them was a tiny hill, covered with grass that was far too lush and green for a winter day. The mound was hardly taller than they were on horseback, and it was perfectly round. Near the top, Terence saw the black opening of a cave, and he shivered involuntarily.

A faint rasping sound came from nearby. Terence had taken care of armor far too long not to recognize it instantly: a whetstone.

"So this is the Green Chapel," Gawain murmured. "An older sort of holy place than I had expected. Come on, Terence." They dismounted and walked around the hill, and there was the Green Knight.

Even larger than Terence remembered, the knight sat on a small three-legged stool, hunched over a small whetstone, sharpening his axe.

"I am here, sir knight," Gawain said.

"Abide your time," the Green Knight said without looking up. "You'll receive everything I promised you." He tested the axe's edge with his finger, then ran it very gently along the whetstone one more time and stood, a satisfied look on his green visage. "It seems that your word holds good, my friend. You have come to *my* court on the correct day."

"I said I would." Gawain bowed.

"Well?" the knight said.

"Well what?" Gawain replied curtly.

"Take off your helm." The knight gestured at a wide stump, large enough for three men to lay their heads on. Gawain nodded and unlaced his helm, handing it to Terence. "And see you make no more demur than I did," the knight added.

Gawain nodded again and knelt at the stump. He smiled cheerfully, which Terence thought was the saddest thing he had ever seen. Terence had to force himself to watch. A tiny muscle high on Gawain's cheekbone twitched, and Gawain clamped his jaw tight, still resolutely smiling. The Green Knight whistled tunelessly and set his feet. Then, still whistling, he lifted the axe high and brought it down.

It never touched Gawain. At the last second, the

Green Knight checked the blow so that it stopped inches from Gawain's neck. Gawain's shoulders quivered ever so slightly, and his smile faded.

"You can't be the glorious Gawain!" the knight jeered. "They say that you've never drawn back from danger in your life, but I say they lie. It seems that I am the better man after all. I ask you, did I flinch like that when you struck me? Did I shrink like a coward away from the axe? Did I?"

"You did not," Gawain said through clenched teeth. His face was flushed with anger, but he only laid his neck on the stump. He no longer smiled: his face wore an odd expression that Terence could not interpret. He nodded curtly to the Green Knight, as if to say "What are you waiting for?"

The knight chuckled merrily and took his stance again. Again he lifted his axe, and again he swung mightily. This time he did not check the blow; the axe sank deep into the stump next to Gawain's motionless neck. Gawain sprang to his feet, fury in his face. "Ah, so you have your nerve again!" the Green Knight said mockingly. "Then let us finish this now, before it escapes you. I do hate to strike a coward. Shall we see if you can uphold the honor of Arthur's court one more time?" Gawain breathed raggedly, eyes flaming with suffused anger. He almost threw himself onto the stump for the third blow. This time when the faery knight raised the axe his face held none of the amusement that had played there the first two times. His lips tightened as he held the axe aloft for a long second, and then he swung the edge down with a fierce grunt.

The stump shivered, and the sound of the axe striking rang out and echoed against the edge of the distant forest. Gawain rolled off the stump. Terence saw a flash of blood on Gawain's neck, and his throat tightened, but then Gawain scrambled to his feet, the Sword Galatine miraculously in his right hand. "You'll get no fourth attempt!" Gawain cried. "I've taken your one blow, and if you wish another, you'll pay for it blow by blow!" Gawain's neck was bright with blood, ebbing from a long scratch, but his feet were steady. Terence held Gawain's helm loosely in one hand, ready to toss it to his master, and he rested the other hand lightly on the hilt of his own sword.

The Green Knight chuckled. He calmly pulled his axe from the stump and leaned carelessly on it. "Now now, my little friend, I see no need for this unseemly display of anger. I've made no untoward demands of you. I owed you a blow, and I gave you a blow. The rest of my rights I freely resign."

"You have no other rights!" Gawain snapped.

"Have I not? I could have done you a good deal of harm, little man. The first stroke I but feinted, for on the first night you were true to our bargain."

Gawain took a step backward, and his eyes widened. The knight continued. "The second time, I missed you entirely, for on that night too you returned to me all that you won that day." A dizzying bewilderment swept over Terence. "But you failed at the third throw, my little friend, and you deserve more than this little tap I've given. Or did you think that I would not know about the green girdle my wife gave you on the third day?"

Gawain's face froze, and his eyes no longer focused on the Green Knight. Slowly the color drained from his face. He dropped his sword to the ground and began to fumble at the laces to his breastplate. Terence saw with astonishment that Gawain's hands were shaking. "Milord?"

"Take off my armor, Terence," Gawain said. He continued to fumble at the knots until Terence gently pushed his fingers away and removed Gawain's breastplate himself. Gawain pulled off the green belt and threw it in front of the Green Knight. "There is the girdle, and may it be cursed, for I purchased it at the cost of my honor." He knelt again at the stump and offered his neck to the Green Knight.

But the Green Knight shook his head. "Nay, Sir Gawain. I've received my due. Now you are indeed worthy."

"Now I am worthy?" The Green Knight nodded

solemnly, and Gawain said, "How can you say that, when I have but now learned my own unworthiness?"

"You have answered yourself, Sir Gawain," the Green Knight said. Gawain bowed his head in dejection. The knight picked up the green girdle and tossed it to Gawain. "Keep this. Wear it always. Like your wound, it is a badge of this test."

"A badge of failure?"

"Failure is easy. This is a badge of shame. Come, Sir Gawain, Terence. We have done at the Green Chapel, and you have far to ride this day."

Gawain looked weary. "But where have we yet to go?"

"Avalon."

The Green Knight would say no more. He disappeared into the cave in the Green Chapel and emerged several minutes later as Sir Bercilak, though the foolish smile that their host had worn for the past week was gone. He whistled once, and his horse trotted out of the little grove by the brook. Gawain said, "Then my quest is not finished."

"You should know that there is always more to the quest than appears in the call," Sir Bercilak said. "Come, friends. I fear that our ladies will grow weary awaiting us."

They rode over a rise, and on the other side Lady

Marion and Eileen were waiting. From Eileen's grim expression, Terence guessed that Lady Marion had already explained to her Gawain's test and how he had failed. She looked wordlessly at Terence, her eyes unnaturally large. Then she turned to Gawain and said, "I can only beg your pardon, Gawain, for advising you to save your life at the expense of your honor."

Terence was glad that she had put it into words, for he had not known how. "Forgive me, too, milord," he said.

Gawain shook his head. "The shame is only mine." Gawain's face was haggard.

"Nay, Sir Gawain," Sir Bercilak laughed. "You take it too hard. You have learned shame, true, but shame need not mean unhappiness. Onward!"

X

THE DUKE OF AVALON

The sun had set behind the hills at their back, and
the shadows of evening already covered Gawain,
Terence, Eileen, and Sir Bercilak. But the island
fortress across the channel before them stood high
out of the sea, the orange evening sunlight still on
it, lighting its white walls with a warm glow. The
castle seemed an island of light in a sea of shadows.
"Avalon," Sir Bercilak said. "And here I shall leave
you. You must face the final tests alone."

"What tests are those?" Gawain asked.

"The Test of the Sea and the Test of the Gate. If
you pass those, I shall see you again. God be with
you." He turned his horse and cantered back up the
darkening hill behind them.

Eileen patted Caesar's neck and asked, "Should
we try to cross now or wait until morning?"

"Wait until morning," Terence suggested, remembering that Gawain's strength would be greater as the sun rose.

Gawain shook his head. "No, who knows if that castle will even be there in the morning? We must go at once."

They rode to the water's edge, but Eileen wheeled Caesar and said sharply, "There's something in there!"

"The Test of the Sea, eh?" Terence said.

As his answer, Gawain pointed at the water's edge. One by one, little sleek heads with human faces popped out of the surf, and little black eyes examined the three riders. Soon there were dozens of them, some almost entirely submerged and some standing in the shallows.

"What are they?" Eileen said.

"They look like seals," Terence said. "But they have arms and legs."

"Ay, lad," Gawain said. "Unless I'm far off, these are the seal-people, what we call the selkies in Orkney."

Several of the selkies pointed back up the mountain and waved their arms urgently. "They seem to want us to leave," Eileen said.

"For our sake or theirs?" Gawain mused. Suddenly, the selkies all disappeared, leaving barely a ripple on the surface of the sea. Gawain and Terence drew their swords and looked around, but there was no danger to be seen on land. Then a different sort of head rose from the surf behind the selkies, revealing the most hideous face Terence had ever seen. It had the usual human features, but everything was grotesquely proportioned. The eyes were huge, round, lidless holes in the head; the nose jutted out a full six inches and spread back across the face almost to the ears; the lipless mouth showed huge yellow teeth that clenched and unclenched spasmodically. The creature's skin was raddled and taut with a crisscross pattern of bare and bleeding muscles, like the weaving on a cane chair. Eileen gasped. The monster raised impossibly long arms, upon which sharp, ragged fin-gers waved like winter twigs, turned its wildly gaping eyes toward them, and screeched "Who...are...you?"

"I am Sir Gawain, of King Arthur's Court, the Maiden's Knight!" Gawain called in reply, in an even, measured voice, as if he were greeting a knight errant on the road.

The thing lurched forward until the water was waistdeep, and Terence saw with surprise that it was on horseback, as the head and shaggy neck of a lean, wild-eyed roan rose from the sea before the creature. "What...do...you...seek...Sir...Gawain?" howled the monster.

"I seek crossing to Avalon. And who are you?"

"I...am...Nuckelavee!" shrieked the creature. Every syllable seemed wrenched from within the thing, as if it were in constant, unbearable pain. "No crossing!" it cried.

Gawain drew his sword and lifted his shield from its latch on his saddle. "Stop me, then!" he called, and he kicked Guingalet into a dead run down the beach. Slavering with delight, Nuckelavee raced forward, out of the water, and Terence realized the monster was not really riding a horse, but instead the raw and sinewy human torso grew out of the center of the horse's back, like a parasite on a tree trunk. They came together with a crash, and Nuckelavee easily plucked Gawain's shield from his grasp. With a horrible scream, the monster began tearing the shield to pieces with its nails, as if the wood and iron were paper.

When Nuckelavee had finished, the monster roared back toward Gawain. This time Gawain dodged in his saddle as the monster came near, and Nuckelavee missed any vital spot, but where its nails had scraped against Gawain's arm the armor was curled and torn. Gawain had slashed with his sword, but on Nuckelavee's skinless sinews it was impossible to see if he had done any harm. Both wheeled and charged together again. Just before they struck, Gawain kicked his feet from the stirrups and lay backwards in his saddle. Nuckelavee's sweeping nails missed Gawain completely, and Gawain caught the monster's arm and swung himself onto its back, just behind the human-like torso. Nuckelavee reared and threw itself on its back in the sand, but Gawain clung tight. It scrambled to its feet, roared from both mouths, and galloped back toward the sea. Gawain's hand, still somehow holding his sword, rose and fell once, then twice, before they crashed into the surf and disappeared below the surface.

Terence and Eileen watched the sea, but they saw nothing. The sun had sunk lower, so that only the topmost turret of the island castle was still lit, and the sea grew blacker every moment. "Do you see anything?" Terence asked hopelessly.

"It's too dark," she said reassuringly. "He's probably out there, but we just can't see him."

Terence called, but there was no answer. "He's fully armored," Terence said. "He can't swim in armor." He slumped to the beach in weary sorrow. Eileen put her hands on his shoulder and stood over him listening. After several minutes, she said, "Something's coming."

Terence stood and raised his sword. If it was Nuckelavee returning, Terence intended to defend Eileen to the death. But it was a slender, lithe person who seemed to rise from the dark water and bring its darkness with him. "It's one of those — what did Gawain call them? — selkies," Terence said.

The selkie stooped, as if bowing, then pointed across the channel toward the island and beckoned. They clearly were supposed to follow. Terence hesitated, looking uncertainly at Eileen. "I can't lead you into danger, Eileen," he said.

"There may be more danger in staying here," Eileen said. "Let's go." They joined hands and stepped into the waves, now almost completely black. Immediately they were caught up by dozens of hands and whisked forward. Terence raised his sword, but even if he chose to fight, there was no one to attack. He and Eileen skimmed along the top of the water, with only their legs actually under the surface, held aloft by the soft hands of the selkies. In less time than he would have believed, Terence found Eileen and himself on the shore of the island. Nearby, gasping and coughing but certainly alive, was Gawain.

Terence laid his sword on the beach and bowed to the selkies. "Thank you," he said. They bowed in deep homage, first to Terence, then to Gawain, and disappeared into the strait.

"Milord?" Terence stooped over his master's shaking form.

Gawain coughed and vomited seawater and then

gazed blankly into Terence's eyes. "Am I back on the beach?"

"No, milord. We're on the island. The selkies brought Eileen and me. And you?" Gawain shrugged weakly. Terence continued, "And Nuckelavee?"

"At the bottom," Gawain whispered. "Dead."

"The Test of the Sea," Eileen said quietly.

Slowly, Gawain stood and looked up the hill at the dark castle. "And now, the Test of the Gate." They waited together on the shore until Gawain's breathing grew even again, then Gawain raised his sword and started up the slope.

Several minutes later, panting from the climb, they came to a mighty wooden gate. Outside the gate, a ring of bright torches formed a circle of orange light. "It seems we're expected," Gawain commented.

From within the high gate came a loud thump, then a horrible creaking, as the gate began to rise. Light spilled from the growing opening. A long human shadow took shape in the blaze of light. It was a knight, in old-fashioned armor.

"Good evening, friend," Gawain said, in greeting. "We are three travelers, come far to this place, who beg admittance."

The knight replied quietly, "Only by killing me can you enter this gate."

"Sir knight, I have no wish to kill you. Is there no other way?"

"There are always other ways, but I know of none. Either leave this island, or prepare now to do battle."

"Then I must do battle," Gawain said. "I am called here. I cannot leave."

"And I," the knight said, "I am called to keep you out." The knight drew his sword and stepped forward. Gawain met him with a bow. "Have you no shield, friend?" the knight asked.

"Nay. It was lost in another battle."

The knight of the gate nodded and threw his own shield behind him. Then the battle was on.

In five years of watching the best swordplay in Britain, Terence had never seen a battle to compare. Again and again, brilliant stroke was countered by brilliant parry. If Gawain's life had not been at stake, Terence would have been enraptured by the beauty and artistry of the combat. The knights fought with swords, with fists, with their bodies. It was now full dark and Gawain's strength was at its lowest point, but he held on. Chips of sliced-off armor littered the ground, and Gawain's armor hung on his frame in stiff, jagged tatters. A full moon rose, and still the battle wore on. An hour passed, then another; the combatants staggered and limped. Each time one knight would muster the strength to launch an attack, the other would somehow find the strength to repulse it.

Twice the two knights fell and lay on the ground

gasping, watching each other. But each time one would finally struggle to his feet, the other would stand as well. Terence began to hope that the fight would continue until dawn, when the sun would give Gawain strength, but the end came just before sunrise. The knight of the gate lunged, slicing downward with his sword, and Gawain's desperate parry struck the knight's gauntleted fist and disarmed him. The knight sank to his knees, almost thankfully. With one move, he removed his helm and bowed his head for the final stroke. The knight's face was lined, and his hair, once black, was silvered with age.

"What do you await, friend?" the knight panted. "Do what you must, and do not regret it."

Gawain lifted his sword, and braced himself, but Terence leaped forward and threw himself on the knight's neck. "No, Gawain! No!" he cried. Gawain lowered his sword. "Look at his neck, Gawain!"

On the side of the knight's bent neck was a long scar. Gawain looked at it blankly. "What do you mean, Terence?"

"It's the same!"

"Same as what?"

"Same as yours! It's identical!"

Gawain's eyes widened, and he gazed at the scar with growing comprehension. "Friend," he asked gently, "how came you by that scar?"

The knight raised his head and met Gawain's gaze. "By failure, friend. By unworthiness and shame."

His fingers trembling slightly, Gawain unlaced his own helm and bared his neck, with its own livid scar. "I too," he said simply. The knight blinked with astonishment. "I shall not kill you, O knight," Gawain said, sheathing his sword. "Truly, it went to my heart to kill you when I thought you only the greatest fighter I had ever known. Now I cannot. Rise, friend." Unsteadily, the knight of the gate stood, and Gawain knelt at his feet.

"It is well done, Sir Gawain," a voice said. "And well done, my Terence. Now you have passed the Test of the Gate." The silhouette of a man stood in the bright, open gateway. The knight of the gate bowed deeply and said, "My lord."

The silhouette turned to the knight and said, "Such a battle has never been seen, in this world or any other. It was well fought, O Cucholinn." Terence and Gawain turned toward the knight with undisguised awe. This was Cucholinn, the hero of the old songs and stories, the child of the sun, the warrior of all ages. "Yes, Sir Gawain," the silhouette said, a smile in his voice, "Cucholinn of the great tales. But in your own world, the tales of Gawain are already surpassing those of Cucholinn. Come, you are weary. A room has been prepared for you in my castle." The silhouette stepped into the light of the torches and Terence and Gawain recognized him at once. It was the great ruler of the faeries that they had met once before in the Other World, Ganscotter the Enchanter. It was Terence's father.

When Gawain and Terence had been to Ganscotter's castle years before, on an earlier quest, Terence had grown to love the gentle, wise, ageless ruler; but he had not known at the time that Ganscotter was his own father. He had learned that several weeks later, from the little messenger Robin. Since then, Terence had longed to see the Enchanter again and embrace him as his son. Now that he actually faced him, though, he was overcome with a sudden shyness. He could only bow beside Gawain at Ganscotter's feet.

Then the Enchanter was gone, and several smiling ladies were helping Gawain, Terence, and Eileen into the castle and installing them in lush, opulent bedchambers. One of the ladies, Lady Audrey, informed them that there would be a banquet that evening in their honor, but that until then they were free to rest as they wished. Terence lay down on his bed and was asleep in seconds. The sun was just rising from the eastern sea.

The shadows were already long from the west when Terence awoke to a tapping on his door. Groggy from sleep, Terence said, "Yes?"

Eileen peeked in. Immediately Terence sat up and

held out his arms. She came to him, and they held each other in silence. Then the silence dissolved as Eileen could no longer wait. "Oh, Terence! Did you recognize him? This is the castle of Ganscotter, the one you told me about, whose castle you visited once before. And I've met his daughter, Lorie, the one you said that Gawain was in love with, and she's wonderful, and did you see the clothes that they've given to me?"

Dutifully, Terence said, "You look very nice."

"Oh, shut up. You didn't even notice," Eileen said merrily, handing Terence a small bundle. "Here are some new clothes for you, too, and you'd better be putting them on, because the banquet begins in a few minutes. They sent me to see if you were awake. Lady Audrey says that an escort will come for us in Gawain's room — right through that door. You dress, and I'll take Gawain's clothes to him."

Terence only nodded. The joy that overflowed in Eileen's delighted chatter also filled his breast, although more quietly. Their quest was over, Gawain was alive, Eileen was near, and Terence was home. He put on the clothes that Eileen had brought and joined her in Gawain's room. It took both of them to rouse him from his sleep, but at last Gawain was up and dressed.

They heard a knock at the door, and Terence opened it. Waiting at the threshold was a tall woman with straight blonde hair. She said, "I have come to escort you to the master's banquet." Either her voice or her face seemed vaguely familiar to Terence. She continued, "The master thought that Squire Terence could escort the Lady Eileen, and he sent me to walk with Sir Gawain, if that is acceptable." The woman smiled toward Gawain, who was staring at her incredulously. The woman's smile deepened, and she said, "Did you think I should be thirteen years old forever, G'winn?"

"Elaine?" Gawain whispered. The woman nodded, and then she threw herself into Gawain's arms. Terence watched the joyful reunion with awe.

"His sister?" Eileen asked. "The one who... died?"

At last the brother and sister broke apart, and Gawain stammered, "But how?"

Elaine said, "On this island it matters little whether you are alive or dead in another world. No other realm has power here. Come, the master is waiting."

Gawain's sister led them to a large, clean, well-lighted hall with vaulted ceilings and, on all sides, great arches that led to other chambers. Through one of these arches, Terence glimpsed a banquet hall, prepared for a feast, but he barely glanced there. His eyes were drawn irresistibly to a dais in the center of the hall. There, on an oaken throne, sat

Ganscotter the Enchanter, and beside him was his daughter Lorie.

Gawain, who had entered ahead of Terence, knelt, and Terence and Eileen joined him. Elaine said, "I have brought my brother to you as you requested, my lord."

"Thank you, my lady," Ganscotter said. "We are pleased beyond measure to entertain Sir Gawain again. You may rise." They all stood, and Ganscotter continued, "When you came before to my castle, the time that you became the Maiden's Knight, I told you that you would have another quest. Now you have completed that second quest, and I must ask you, Sir Gawain, what you have learned from all the trials you have overcome."

Gawain paused, collecting his thoughts, then said, "I have learned that I am weak and selfish, that I am willing to trade my honor for my life — which, here on this island, seems an insignificant prize. I am ashamed."

Ganscotter raised one eyebrow. "Ashamed? But what of your many victories? What about your defeat of the boar-headed knight? What of your battle with the great Cucholinn?"

"Whatever glory I earn by such victories will soon be forgotten in another hero's story."

"Very true," said Ganscotter with a smile. "You

have done well and have earned a prize. Have you any request?"

Gawain nodded. "I have long wished to marry your daughter, if she will have me."

Ganscotter smiled. "I cannot say nay. Lorie?"

In a low, gorgeous voice that made Terence catch his breath, Lorie said, "I will have you, Sir Gawain."

Ganscotter turned to Eileen. "Welcome, Lady Eileen, to my court. Forgive me that I have not introduced myself before. I am Ganscotter the Enchanter, a ruler among the faeries, and your servant." Speechless, Eileen could only curtsy. Ganscotter continued. "You have come a great distance with these travelers. Such faithfulness deserves a reward. Will you allow me to grant you a wish?" Eileen stared, incomprehending, and Ganscotter said, "What is your heart's desire?"

Eileen curtsied again, then said, "Sir, my lord, I ... I have what I desire."

"What is that, daughter?"

"I have found friendship and love, sir. Sir Gawain has become my friend, and I have learned to love his squire, Terence."

Ganscotter frowned. "Lady Eileen, you are of noble birth, the granddaughter of a noble duke. Is it seemly for you to give your love to a mere squire?"

At Ganscotter's words, Terence blinked in surprise,

and Gawain started to protest, but Lady Eileen replied, "I don't care, sir. I love Terence. I have seen him do great things, and all his mighty deeds have been to protect someone else."

Ganscotter broke into a smile and stepped forward off the dais. "I'm proud of him, too, Eileen," he said. Then, eyes streaming with tears, Ganscotter took Terence in his arms and said, "Well done, my son."

Terence could not speak for the tears that choked him. He could say nothing while Ganscotter embraced him, nor when the Enchanter announced to all present — to the shock of both Gawain and Eileen — that Terence was indeed his true son. He could not even speak when Ganscotter touched his son's shoulder with a gleaming sword and proclaimed him Sir Terence, Knight of the Island, Duke of Avalon, and led him to the banquet hall, to the place of honor at Ganscotter's right hand.

XI

To the World of Men

They spent many days at Avalon, though no one cared to count the exact number. Gawain and Lorie were married with great solemnity and gladness. Terence spent hours with Eileen, but he found time for others as well, especially for his family. For the first time in his memory, Terence was part of a family. Although Terence had met Ganscotter and Lorie before, he had not known then that they were his father and sister. Moreover, since Gawain and Lorie were married, his master and best friend was now also his brother-in-law. Terence suddenly had a family, a best friend, and a beloved lady who returned his love. To one raised as a foundling in a secluded hermitage, affection from so many sides was almost bewildering.

Terence talked much with his father, learning the ways of the Other World. The Enchanter told Terence about his magic and about the stronger, and kinder, magic that lay even beyond his own. Often they spoke of love, for Ganscotter, too, had known love like Terence's. One day, high on the castle walls, Ganscotter told Terence about his own experiences. He spoke first of the regal French princess who had been Lorie's mother. "I thought when she died that my heart would never feel again," he said. "Until I met a gentle peasant girl from Yorkshire. Your mother."

"What was my mother like?" Terence asked shyly.

Ganscotter looked over the misty fields below, as if seeing across the worlds. "Her cheeks were always red and warm, even before the first fire was lit on a frosty winter morning; her lips were never far from smiling. Though she was young, her eyes already had the wrinkles at the corners that distinguish a merry life. I wanted to give her everything, but I never gave her as much as she gave me." Ganscotter looked at Terence and said, "Your face is the face of a faery, my son. But your selfless heart is the gift of your mother. As always, she has given more than I."

"You told me the last time that I was here that she died when I was a baby," Terence said carefully. Ganscotter nodded, and Terence continued. "Why, then, was I left in that other place, the World of Men?"

For a long time, Ganscotter did not answer, and when he did, Terence thought at first that the Enchanter was changing the subject. Ganscotter said, "You have now seen two different worlds, Terence, and have been a part of both. You have seen that they are different, have you not?" Terence nodded and the Enchanter continued. "In this world, there is good and bad, but not like in the World of Men. In that world, badness quickly becomes monstrous evil, and goodness — well, goodness can become sublime."

"Why?" asked Terence.

"Humans are just different. No other creatures have the capacity for such evil and such folly. That is why the rare human who is truly good — like your mother — is so remarkable. And the rare human who aquires true wisdom — like King Arthur — is so magnificent."

"Yes, sir," Terence said. "But you haven't explained —"

"Patience, child. Because of the weight of human foolishness, some kinds of magic are rare in that world. For instance, we faeries may travel between worlds easily, but those born of human flesh may not. That includes you. Though you were my own son, I could not bring you to this world until you were old enough to put aside the selfishness and folly that all humans inherit."

"And so you left me with the hermit, Trevisant," Terence said.

"I knew of no one who could teach you so well. And in your humble service to Trevisant and to your master, you have now proven yourself."

They were silent for several minutes. "Sir?" Terence asked suddenly, "If I had not had faery blood, would I have been able to cross to this world?"

Ganscotter shook his head. "No. No one who is entirely human may make this crossing." Terence thought at once of Eileen, and Ganscotter, as if reading his mind, added, "Yes, even Eileen has a trace of faery blood, by way of Ireland. You might say she is a distant cousin to a leprechaun."

"I might," Terence said, grinning. "But not to her face. I love her, but I'm not a complete fool."

Ganscotter smiled but replied immediately. "No one who loves is a complete fool. Or if so, it is a divine foolishness."

The phrase sounded familiar, and Terence searched his memory for it. Then he remembered. "Gawain said something like that to Arthur before we left." Terence hesitated, then asked, "Was Gawain right? Is Arthur's love for Guinevere divine —or just foolish?"

Ganscotter shook his head noncommittally. "The outcome remains to be seen. But it is not wrong for

Arthur to love, even though he loves someone who is neither smart enough nor courageous enough to love him in kind."

Thinking of Arthur's stubborn faithfulness to Guinevere, and imagining how he would feel himself if Eileen gave her love to another, Terence felt a deep indignation. "What more could Guinevere want than Arthur's love?" he demanded.

"It is not that she wants more, child. It is that she wants less. Arthur's love for her exceeds reason, surpasses all the prescribed rules, and it frightens her. Lancelot courts her according to the rules."

"What rules?"

"The rule that handsome men and beautiful women must always love each other. The rule that men show their love for women by defeating other men. The rule that love is won as one wins tournaments, by proving yourself the most beautiful. The rule that love for a famous person is nobler than love for a humble person."

Terence frowned. "But those rules are rubbish."

"Yes."

"I wish I could help him," Terence murmured.

"You can," Ganscotter said. Terence looked up, but Ganscotter shook his head. "No, I cannot tell you how. But you will have your chance when you return to Camelot." Terence stared at Ganscotter in dismay, and the Enchanter said gently, "Avalon is your home, but you are not to stay here forever this time. Remember only that you will never leave here forever."

Terence's dismay at hearing that he had to leave his true home was nothing to Gawain's when he heard that he had to leave his true love. For long minutes, Gawain stared bleakly at the wall of his bedchamber while Terence wished he could remove his master's grief. Terence wanted to repeat Ganscotter's words —"You will never leave here forever"—but it was not a time for words, so he only shared his master's silence.

When at last the day came for their departure, the three friends were as ready as they could be. Gawain was no more reconciled to leaving Lorie, but he had accepted that the parting was temporary. The three travelers prepared for a journey, as they had so many times before, and bid tearful goodbyes. They boarded a shining ferry of pearl and floated across to the opposite shore, where to no one's surprise they found their gear and horses awaiting them on the beach.

"So," Eileen said, "which direction?"

Gawain, still lost in his grief at parting, did not reply, so Terence said, "Go back the same way we came, I suppose, and hope it's easier this time around."

They did not get far before they were stopped. As they approached a forest, a slim green figure, about three feet tall, stepped from the trees. It was Robin.

"Good day, Sir Gawain!" Robin called, bowing toward Gawain. "Bid you good morrow, Lady Eileen!" Last of all, he turned toward Terence and bowed until his nose touched the ground, saying, "And all salutations to your grace, the Duke of Avalon."

Terence grinned, and Gawain, distracted from his reverie, bowed slightly in return and asked, "And whom do I have the honor to address?"

"Only one of the humblest of your admirers, Sir Gawain," Robin said meekly.

"Stow it, Robin," Terence said. "And don't call me your grace. How've you been?"

Robin chuckled. "Passing well, Terence. Passing well."

Gawain raised his eyebrows in surprise. "You know this fellow, Terence?"

"Ay. This is Robin, the messenger I've told you about."

"I see," Gawain nodded. "You say your name is Robin, eh? Have you another name?"

"At least a dozen, Sir Gawain."

"Would one of them be Goodfellow?"

Robin chuckled slyly. "Some have called me so, though I'm not certain why."

"Robin Goodfellow, whom some call Puck. Am I right?"

"It's not my favorite name."

Gawain went on. "The Puck of whom I have heard is an imp, a mischievous sprite who'd rather cause trouble than eat, a merry little good-for-nothing whose greatest delight is to make fools of humans."

"Ay, that's the fellow," Terence agreed.

Robin looked pleased, but he murmured, "As if humans needed my help."

"Well, good Robin, how may we serve you?" Gawain asked.

"No no, Sir Gawain. I've come to serve you. I'm to lead you back to the World of Men." He led a little white pony out of the trees, mounted, and pointed them west.

Soon they came upon Sir Bercilak, armed and mounted, waiting for them by a brook. His face wreathed with smiles, he greeted them all, including Robin, as long-lost friends. Gawain was rapidly recovering his composure and was able to smile his own greeting. "Do you ride with us, Sir Bercilak?"

"It would be unseemly for the Maiden's Knight, the Duke of Avalon, and the renowned Lady Eileen of Wirral to ride without an honor guard," Bercilak said.

Terence whistled. "Lady Eileen of Wirral," he murmured admiringly.

"I like it," Eileen said, tossing her head pertly. "You're not the only one who can have a toplofty title, after all."

They rode quickly, passing many places they recognized from the outward journey. They seemed to cover in a day distances that had taken them weeks before. The wind was always at their back, their horses never grew weary, and the ground itself seemed eager to fly beneath their horses' hooves and lose itself behind them. At the end of a week, they came to the edge of the woods and rode out onto the vast plain along the river. In the distance, Terence could make out the misty outline of the mountain they had climbed the night they crossed into the World of Faeries.

"Oh, look!" Eileen exclaimed, pointing at a lush grotto at the edge of the forest, resplendent with flowers. "Oh, you can smell them from here!" she cried. "Why did we not see this on our way?"

"Ah, but you did, my lady," Robin said. "Do you not recognize it?"

Terence saw nothing that he recognized, but after a moment, Eileen said, "Terence, do you see a house of some kind in the heart of that jumble of flowers there?"

"Maybe," he admitted.

"Robin, is this the hovel of that dreadful Annis?" Eileen demanded.

"It is that." He grinned. "See what a difference you've made here, my lady?"

"It's delightful!" she pronounced. "I should like to spend the night here, Robin."

"As you wish," he replied. Thus it was that they went to sleep surrounded by flowers: breathing their perfume and cushioned by their petals. Seldom had Terence fallen asleep more easily, but shortly after midnight he awoke, uneasy but unafraid. Careful not to disturb anyone, he took his sword to the darkness at the edge of the camp. Just in the shadows, Robin sat on a stump.

"There, to the left," Robin whispered. Terence looked where the sprite indicated. Rising slowly from the river was a bluish mist, an eerie-looking, irregular sort of fog, and at the edge of the fog, seeming almost to drag it behind, a dark shape shuffled along the riverbank. Terence lifted his sword. "Who is it, Robin?"

"Hag Annis, of course."

Terence jumped. "Alive?"

"Not really. Nor really dead. You have seen that death is not always the horror that it is thought in the World of Men. Hag Annis is forbidden death and must stay forever in the in-between."

Terence shivered. "How horrible," he said. He watched the sad, shuffling figure disappear in the blackness.

The next day, they met the stranger whom Gawain had wrestled. He rose like a ghost from the plain beside their path and greeted them joyfully. "Knight! You've come back!"

"I have, friend." Gawain smiled. He gestured at Sir Bercilak and Terence and said, "These are knights, too."

"I want to be a knight," the stranger said seriously. Terence grinned. A very single-minded fellow this was.

"Come with me, and you shall have your chance," Gawain said.

"Who can make me a knight?"

"King Arthur himself, King of All Britain."

"I must bid goodbye to my mother," the stranger said, pensively. "Is this King Arthur hard to find?"

"In the World of Men, all know of Arthur."

"I shall find him, then."

Gawain bowed. "As you wish, friend. I shall tell him to expect you. What, may I ask, is your name?"

"I am Parsifal," the stranger said. Gawain took formal leave of Parsifal, and the little cavalcade continued along the plain, into the rocks and up to the mountain.

They passed the road where they met the pilgrim, then began the steep climb up the mountain itself. Before they had gone halfway, Terence began to see little people peeking at them from behind rocks and trees. He was alarmed at first, but these little people—none of them any larger than Robin—did not seem at all dangerous. The men had beards, and the women wore shawls. Almost all were fat.

"Who the devil are these?" Gawain laughed.

"I think they're darling!" Eileen said.

Robin chuckled. "Perhaps so, my lady, but it will only offend them if you say so. Of course, they may say something of the sort about you."

"Oh, will we talk to them?" she asked.

"Dear me, yes," he replied. "By now they're all waiting for you at the top."

"Is there any danger, good Robin?" Gawain asked.

Robin laughed. "You'll never find a more peaceable sort than the mountain folk."

Then they rode into the meadow where they had camped and recovered from their wounds, and just over the crest of the hill Terence saw the gently rising smoke of village fires. It was the elfin village. At the top of the mountain, they reined in and looked down on the town. There was the square where they had fought the boar-man and the wild boars, but it was no longer deserted. Dozens of little people filled the courtyard, cheering shrilly.

"So what's all this in aid of?" Gawain asked Robin.

"Didn't you guess? You freed their village from the boar-knight. They've named the well after you."

"How did they know my name?"

"They don't. They invented one." Gawain looked at Robin warily, and, eyes dancing, Robin said, "Sir Wozzell. It seemed to them a most heroic name. The mountain folk are not especially clever, perhaps I should mention."

At that moment, the crowd of elves surged forward, shouting hysterically, "Sir Wozzell! Sir Wozzell!" Half of them clamored around Gawain and half around Sir Bercilak. Forced on by an irresistible tide of little bodies, the travelers moved slowly down the hill into the square. It was odd how the empty, frightening elfin village of that night seemed so pleasantly innocuous when filled with its amiable residents. On a balcony, a formally attired man wearing several bright sashes pompously gave a speech in which Terence occasionally made out the words "welcome," "honored," and "privilege," but which was largely drowned out by the shouting of the crowds. No one, not even the one giving it, seemed to mind that the speech was being lost. Robin calmly urged his horse through the crowd, opening a wake for the others to follow. A few minutes later, they were through the crowd, which did not seem to notice their absence.

Gawain looked back over his shoulder at the celebration. "How did they know that I was the one who saved them?"

"They don't." Robin chuckled. "You're the third knight they've celebrated over since it happened."

"So they rejoice over every knight they meet?"

"Of course. You can't have too many Sir Wozzells."

They rode a few more steps, to the grassy edge of the precipice which they had climbed. Off in the distance Terence saw the towns and castles and villages and farmlands of the World of Men. Sir Bercilak touched Gawain's shoulder lightly, smiled, and said, "There is your world, my friend."

"No. Here is my world. But I go to that one."

"As you say. Godspeed, and wear well the badge of your shame. Goodbye, Lady Eileen. Go with God, my lord duke." And then he turned his horse and cantered into the woods, which swallowed him as if he had never been.

Robin touched Terence's elbow and said, "I too must leave you, your grace."

Terence looked down into the impish green face which had guided — or chased — him through so many adventures, and he nodded sadly. "I shall miss you," he said.

Robin chuckled. "You know that the faeries never let go of their own. Watch for me, won't you, your grace?"

"Don't call me your grace," Terence said.

Robin did not answer. Instead, he wheeled his horse and galloped in a close circle around the three travelers. Three times he circled them, and by the third circuit, Terence felt as dizzy as if he had himself been twirling, and the rocks of the mountain spun wildly around him. A merry chuckle floated over the spinning, and then, slowly, the world righted itself before his eyes, and they were in a little clearing in a pleasant sunlit forest. The mountain was nowhere to be seen.

"We're back, aren't we?" Eileen asked after a moment.

"I suppose so," Terence said.

"I wonder how long we've been gone this time," Gawain said lightly. He explained to Eileen. "Last time we were in the World of Faeries, we thought we had been gone for a night, and when we returned, three months had passed."

"I suppose we could ask that knight," Eileen said innocently. Gawain and Terence followed her gaze across the clearing to where a mounted knight sat on his horse watching them. "Naturally, you two famous knights noticed that we were being watched," she added demurely.

"Shrew," Terence said with a chuckle.

"Shall we greet the fellow?" Gawain said, leading the way.

The knight had been hard-used, Terence thought as they neared. His armor was chipped and cut and to Terence's experienced eye showed evidence of much repair. The knight's hair was long and uncut, and a thick beard hung over his breastplate. He made no hostile move, but his left hand rested on his sword hilt, and Terence quietly trotted his horse between the knight and Eileen. Behind the knight, in the shadow of some trees was another horse, on which was either a large pack or a very short rider.

When they were about ten yards away, the bearded knight made a choking noise and leaned forward intently. His hand twitched once, as if to cross himself. Gawain stopped and said, "Well met, fellow. Can you tell us where we are?"

As if he had trouble breathing, the knight gasped, "Are you alive?"

"Ay, to the best of my knowledge," Gawain answered pleasantly. The knight made no reply, and after a second Gawain ventured, "Do I know you, sir knight?"

Dumbly the knight nodded, and then the second horse stepped out of the woods, ridden by a grey-haired dwarf who stared at Gawain and Terence with awe. Terence grinned happily, and Gawain shouted with delight as they recognized the two. It was Tor and Plogrun.

Gawain and Terence threw themselves laughing

onto their old friends. Plogrun shrank away from Terence's embrace, and when Terence finally clasped him, the dwarf's body was rigid. Terence laughed louder, "Come now, duffer! Do you think me a boggart, then?" He leaned close to Plogrun's face and whispered, "Boo."

Slowly, the dwarf's face crinkled into a huge smile. "By Gor, it is you, isn't it? Alive and well, too! By Gor! By Gor!"

"Where are my manners?" Gawain called. "Lady Eileen, allow me to present you to Sir Tor, one of the greatest—and at the moment almost certainly the shabbiest—of all Arthur's knights."

Tor trotted forward and bowed gracefully in his saddle. "Indeed, I apologize for my appearance, Lady Eileen. I have been questing for many months."

"I perfectly understand, Sir Tor," Eileen replied, extending her hand. "And it was poorly done of Sir Gawain to mention it." Tor laughed and raised Eileen's hand to his lips.

"And this, Ei—ah—Lady Eileen," Terence interrupted, "is Tor's squire. Saving myself, the best squire there is. Lady Eileen, Squire Plogrun." Plogrun glanced curiously at Terence, as Terence remembered too late that at court a squire would never put himself forward during formal introductions.

"Thank you, Squire Terence," Eileen said quickly, filling the awkward pause. "Squire Plogrun, I hope that while we ride together — as I trust we will — we may lay aside the more stifling court customs." She smiled brightly, and Plogrun bowed as low as his short torso allowed. Terence grinned at Eileen over Plogrun's head and mouthed, "Thank you."

"By heaven," Tor said, "you two don't look a day older than when you left."

"How much older should we look?" Gawain asked innocently.

Tor was not deceived. "Don't you know?"

Gawain grinned ruefully and shook his head. "We were very busy and lost track of the time."

"It's been seven years since you set out. There's been no word of you since that soldier you sent from the — what was it? The Chateau Wirral — a few weeks after you left. Everyone believes you dead."

Tor's voice had a hint of reproach in it, and dejectedly Gawain said, "Sorry."

"No, you're not, so stop bamming it," Tor said. "Why didn't you send a message? For that matter, what have you been doing that no one's heard of you?"

"Oh, nothing much," Gawain said. "And what are you up to? What's the quest this time, eh?"

"Well you should ask. It's the same quest I've been on every year since you left. I'm hunting your headless mortal remains."

Gawain chuckled, but assumed a dejected face.

"Terribly sorry. If only I'd known."

Tor smiled. "Ah, but I've missed you, lad."

They were, it turned out, seven days from Camelot, and the week on the road did much to restore Terence to a sense of his position. Of course he was a knight now, not to mention a duke, but in the World of Men he was content to revert to being a humble squire, if only he could recall what a humble squire was like. It was with some difficulty that Terence remembered to stay in the background and hold his tongue. Most difficult of all was keeping his distance from Eileen. Both Tor and Plogrun assumed that Eileen was Gawain's lady, and for simplicity's sake, the three friends allowed them to think it. Only after everyone else was asleep were Terence and Eileen able to snatch a few whispered words.

The little cavalcade created a sensation at Camelot. When they arrived at the gate, and Tor called jovially for the guards to open for Sir Gawain, Lady Eileen, and Sir Tor, the astonished soldiers could only stare. The travelers had to wait until the Captain of the Guard himself arrived to let them in. The tall captain grinned and bowed deeply before Sir Gawain. "I have prayed nightly for your safety, Sir Gawain," he said simply.

"Then I am once again in your debt," Gawain said with a smile. It was Alan, the soldier from the

Chateau Wirral. He winked at Terence, bowed to Eileen, then stepped aside.

And then there was Arthur. He stood alone in a doorway across the courtyard, his cheeks wet with tears. He wore no crown, and his clothing was simple and unadorned. His beard was streaked with a few faint lines of grey, and the corners of his eyes were more deeply lined than Terence remembered, but the majesty of his presence was stronger than ever. Eileen whispered, "That's King Arthur." It was not a question. "Oh, Terence, I love him!"

Gawain threw himself from Guingalet and ran across the courtyard to the king, Terence and Eileen following close behind. Gawain knelt at Arthur's feet and murmured, "My liege."

Arthur looked at Gawain for a long moment, then, to the astonishment of all, knelt before Gawain, paying Gawain the same homage that Gawain had paid him. "My friend!" he whispered brokenly. Terence beamed with delight, partly at the honor done to his friend, and partly at the grandeur of this king, a king so majestic that he could bow before one of his subjects and only increase his dignity. The crowd, hushed for a moment, burst into lusty cheers, and the king stood, raising Gawain with him.

"This very evening," Arthur declared, signaling for silence, "we shall begin the feast honoring Sir Gawain." The crowd began to cheer again, but

Arthur stilled them. "We shall feast for three days, and on the fourth, we shall hold the most magnificent tournament that this court has ever seen! Send couriers throughout the land! Summon my huntsmen! All shall be of the very finest, for this one whom we love, who went away to die for our sake, has returned!"

As soon as the hurrahs had subsided, Gawain presented Eileen to the king. She blushed rosily as she curtsied, but Arthur's unfeigned pleasure in welcoming her soon put her at her ease. He led her to his chief housekeeper, saying that Mrs. Grimby would see to her needs until the banquet began that evening. Terence watched her disappear in the crowd then turned back to Gawain, who was grinning happily at the formidable bulk of Sir Kai, which had loomed up beside the king.

"We've missed you, lad," Sir Kai said abruptly. Only the light in his eyes and the slight upward turn of one corner of his mouth betrayed the emotion behind this curt welcome. "We've kept your chambers for you."

Gawain lifted his eyebrows, and Arthur said gently, "I believe I told you once that it is never too much to hope."

XII

THE GREATEST KNIGHT
IN ENGLAND

There were more speeches and welcomes, but as
soon as he was able, Terence slipped away from the
throng. He made his way to the Squires' Court,
the kitchens, and the stables, talking with all the
court servants he found. Three hours later, he
tapped lightly at the door to Gawain's chambers and
slipped in. Gawain had escaped from his admirers
and was alone, stretched out luxuriously in a deep
cushioned chair. "Get lost?" he asked.

"Just taking a look around."

Gawain grinned. "Naturally. What's the news?"

"Sir Lancelot this, Sir Lancelot that. The fellow's
been busy. He's been off on a few quests, saved the
lives of just about every knight at the table at some
time or another, even Sir Kai's."

Gawain raised one eyebrow. "How'd that happen?"

"Story's a bit mangled, but it seems a chap named Sir Turquin started capturing the knights of the Round Table, starting a collection maybe, and even took Sir Kai. Sir Lancelot killed Sir Turquin and set them free." Gawain pursed his lips thoughtfully, and Terence continued. "You remember that fellow Sir Oneas, the one I popped off his horse with my cudgel? Lancelot killed him. They say this Sir Oneas was a regular demon, a knight of passing great prowess or some such rot. Only Lancelot could have defeated so fearsome a fighter, they say."

"That's the story, eh? What else?"

"Your brother's at Camelot."

"Gareth?"

"Ay, that's the fellow."

Gawain raised his eyebrows at the note of disapproval in Terence's voice. "Glad he's here," he said mildly. "I always thought he had potential."

"They say that he's second only to Sir Lancelot. He's been off on a quest and saved all manner of ladies." Gawain grinned with a hint of pride, and Terence coughed slightly. "He...um...didn't want Arthur to knight him, they say."

"He didn't want...? Why not?"

"Thought it would mean more if Sir Lancelot did it."

"Impertinent whelp." Gawain waved his hand in a vague gesture of dismissal. "Lancelot and Guinevere still together?"

Terence only nodded, but then he said, "When you say Guinevere, do you mean the queen?"

Gawain scowled. "Who else would I mean?"

"I'm sure I don't know, milord. The queen isn't referred to by that name anymore. Sir Lancelot has christened her, 'Peerless Perfection of Maidenhood,' and that's what they call her now."

Gawain's frown lightened. "'Peerless Perfection of Maidenhood'? People really call her that?"

"So it seems. Among the people who speak to her at all, only the king still calls her by name."

"'Peerless...' How embarrassing," Gawain said, amused. "I could almost be sorry for her."

At the banquet that night, Terence almost felt sorry for Guinevere himself, starting with his first sight of the queen. She was seven years older now than when they had left on their quest, and the years showed. A few fine wrinkles had appeared at the corners of her eyes. She may have been more pale, too, but it was hard to tell through the blush that she had painted on her cheeks. Eileen, entering the hall just ahead of Terence, leaned back and whispered, "Is *that* the Peerless Perfection of Maidenhood?"

"Oh, you've heard that, have you?"

"Sort of heavily painted, isn't she?"

"It's hard for a Maiden to keep up Peerless Perfection, you know," Terence replied sternly.

Eileen sat beside Gawain, who was at Arthur's right hand, and Terence stood correctly behind Gawain. On Arthur's left, Sir Lancelot maintained a steady flow of extravagant compliments to Guinevere, who accepted them with silence. Terence whispered to Eileen, "I'm surprised the queen can stand to listen to such stuff."

"Maybe she can't," Eileen replied. "But what can she do? It would be hard for a lady to refuse the attentions of the greatest knight in England."

On the first night of the banquet, Tor told about his quest to find Gawain. While his search had little to do with Gawain's return, he had had several harrowing adventures, and it made for interesting listening. When he was done, all present murmured their approval, and Arthur thanked him for adding once again to the glory of the Round Table. On the second night, Gawain began his story. At Terence's insistence, Gawain all but left his squire out of the story. He said nothing of teaching Terence the knightly arts, but rather began his tale with Sir Oneas, the Knight of the Crossroads. Terence kept his face bland while Gawain lavishly described Sir Oneas's great size, terrible fierceness, and surpassing brilliance in arms. Sir Lancelot nodded in solemn agreement.

Gawain then told of his supernatural struggle with the demonic Huntsman of Anglesey, and he laid it on even thicker, telling how the huntsman breathed fire and hurled trees and so on. Gawain thanked Sir Lancelot for the holy shield of Our Lady of Anglesey, which had saved him from the Huntsman's evil darts, and Sir Lancelot, much moved, said not to mention it.

Gawain's account of his escape from the Chateau Wirral was, if not highly accurate, at least very thrilling. In Gawain's story, it was Eileen herself, rather than Terence in one of Eileen's dresses, who freed Gawain from the dungeons. Eileen seemed surprised to learn how heroic she had been, but she bowed modestly. "Indeed," Gawain said, gazing mistily into the distance, "it was a vision of all that is fair in womanhood that greeted my eyes when the dungeon door swung open. Such surpassing loveliness and grace!" Terence grunted, and Eileen's shoulders shook. Gawain concluded by thanking Eileen for her unfailing courage and courtesy, then added, "I hope, indeed I know, that you shall find a knight more worthy than I to cherish you."

This last statement caused a mild sensation in the banquet hall. Like Tor and Plogrun, all Camelot had assumed that Eileen was Gawain's lady, and as soon as they realized their mistake, more than one knight began watching Eileen with unusual interest.

Terence counted at least six knights that would be languishing at Eileen's feet before the week was out, paying her extravagant compliments, and more than likely writing French sonnets to her nose. Gawain gave Terence a twinkling, mischievous glance, and Terence began a mental list of crude names to call his friend when they were alone.

Gawain resumed his story the third night, but he told few of their adventures in the Other World. Omitting the elfin village, he told only of his midnight struggle with Parsifal and of Eileen's escape from Hag Annis. Then, in a serious tone, he told of Bercilak's Keep. He told the whole story, without elaboration or omission. He spoke bluntly of his own cowardice and selfishness in keeping the green girdle that he thought would save his own life. The room grew unnaturally silent as Gawain told of the Green Chapel and how he discovered his own shame.

"I loved my life more than my honor," he said, standing and opening his surcoat to reveal the green girdle against his tunic—"this girdle I wear as a badge of that shame, the shame that will never leave me. This," he finished quietly, taking his seat again, "is my quest."

Terence smiled approvingly. Of course, Gawain could not tell about Avalon, where his shame had been affirmed and his honor restored. Gawain's decision to stop his tale at the Green Chapel was exactly right. By mocking the adventures that would usually be considered worthy and baldly telling of his disgrace, Gawain had told a story that was remarkably different from other knightly tales. It was as if Gawain were himself a messenger from another world.

"This is a marvelous fine tale, sire," a voice rang out in the banquet hall. To Terence's surprise, it was Sir Lancelot. He continued, "Told by a marvelous fine knight."

"Yea, indeed," said another, and then the hall was filled with calls of agreement.

"To wage such battle with the great Sir Oneas!" one said.

"The unnatural Huntsman!" declared another. "What fury! What puissance!"

A young knight wearing a beige hat that was trimmed with lavender lace and looked rather like an elderberry pie, added, "And Lady Eileen! Such purity! So delicate a flower!" He turned what was undoubtably intended as a meaningful look onto Eileen, who nodded politely but who did not appear to Terence to relish being called delicate.

"My king!" Sir Lancelot spoke again, and the hall grew still. "I suggest we do worship to this knight and his marvelous power by instituting a new order of knighthood in his honor!"

Again the hall erupted with loud declarations of

agreement. Gawain leaned forward in his chair and looked curiously at Sir Lancelot. "The Order of the Puissant Sword!" one called out.

"Nay! The Order of the Destroyer of Giants!" another declared.

"Giants?" Gawain blinked. "Where...?"

"Nay!" Sir Lancelot decreed. "The Order of the Green Girdle! What say you, O King?"

Arthur stood, and the hubbub subsided. "Indeed, I believe such an order should be instituted, an order unlike any other. But I wonder if that is truly what you all wish. What does the court say should be the requirements for membership in this new order?"

"Only the very finest of the knights of the Table Round!" Sir Lancelot said immediately.

"Anyone who wins a tournament?" someone else suggested.

"Nay, two tournaments!"

"Three!"

"How about one who kills a giant?"

"Two giants!"

"Anyone Lady Eileen desires," the young knight wearing the pie declared belligerently.

"Nay, anyone Sir Lancelot desires!" called another.

"Three giants!"

"Lady Eileen!"

"Sir Lancelot!"

"What about a knight who has served for five years or more?"

"Or five years and one tournament?"

"Lady Eileen!"

"Four giants!"

"Sir Lancelot!"

"What about one giant and two tournaments?"

"Plus five years of service!"

"What if you can't find a giant?"

"Five years and two tournaments?"

As the shouts grew louder, Arthur turned and looked sadly at Gawain, who was gazing around the room in consternation. Gawain met his eyes with an agonized appeal, but Arthur only shook his head. Sir Lancelot broke into the clamor. "Peace!" The banquet hall grew silent. "All of these are good ideas," he began, "and I feel certain that Sir Gawain agrees."

"No, I don't!" Gawain snapped, but Arthur laid a hand on his shoulder to silence him.

"It is perhaps too much to ask all knights to achieve what Sir Gawain has achieved," Arthur said. His hand, still resting on Gawain's shoulder, tightened expressively. "I know few who could discover such an adventure or tell such a tale." He smiled gently. "Shall we say that any knight who has completed one quest and won the prize at two tournaments may enter the Order of the Green Girdle?"

The knights and ladies gathered there signified their assent by nodding their heads judiciously, as though that was just what they had suggested themselves. Arthur took his seat, and Gawain whispered to him urgently, "My liege, this girdle marks my disgrace, not my feats of arms. I didn't do half of what I told you!"

Arthur smiled and said softly, "Nor, I suspect, did you tell us half of what you did."

"But you can't make the green girdle a reward for doing a certain number of little tasks! It's to make it a treat given to trained dogs!"

Arthur looked fondly at the knights before him. "Not dogs, Gawain: children."

Gawain gave the king a curious, resigned look, and said, "Must I join the new order?"

Arthur shook his head. "Your part in it will be forgotten in a week."

The next day, King Arthur hosted the tournament. As he had promised, it was the most splendid tournament ever seen, and knights came from miles around to participate. Indeed, so many knights were present that Terence heard more than one courtier say that the winner of this contest would truly earn the title "The Greatest Knight in England." If so, then Gawain was not the greatest. He did well enough, of course, even unhorsing his renowned younger brother Gareth, but shortly thereafter was unseated himself by Sir Lancelot. Terence, watching from the end of the ladies' pavilion, could not help feeling a twinge of disappointment, but he found it hard to take a tournament joust very seriously.

A female voice at his shoulder said pleasantly, "I told him once that there was always a better knight." Terence turned to see Morgan Le Fay. He bowed immediately, but when he straightened again she looked at him sharply and said, "Now why is it that I feel that I should be bowing to you?"

"Please do not, my lady," Terence said hastily.

In a minute, Gawain joined them, holding Guingalet's reins. "Why hello, Auntie. When did you arrive?"

"In time to see you take that fall, nephew."

Gawain grinned. "Oh, ay, a lovely sight, no doubt. I can feel my reputation slipping away as we speak. I dare say in a few years I'll be the recreant knight that everyone remembers having unhorsed one time." He chuckled.

"It doesn't seem to concern you," Morgan said, lifting one eyebrow.

"Know any reason it should?"

Morgan stared at Gawain for a moment, then said, "This modesty hardly becomes someone from our family. It must be senility."

"Perhaps so," Gawain said mischievously. "I must trust your greater experience."

Morgan's eyes flashed, but she bowed to Gawain and said graciously, "I believe that takes the trick. I can only retreat."

She turned to leave, and Gawain said, "Morgan?" She glanced over her shoulder, and Gawain said, "I saw Elaine."

Morgan froze. "Little Elaine?" Gawain nodded, and Morgan said, "And?"

"It is well with her."

Morgan nodded once. "Thank you," she said softly, and then she left.

Gawain strolled into a refreshment tent, and Terence turned toward the king's pavilion, where Eileen sat as Arthur's honored guest.

"Nay, your grace," came a pleasant voice behind him. "Come this way, please." Terence recognized Robin's voice, but the demure page boy that he saw when he turned bore no resemblance to the elf. The boy smiled cherubically and said, "I told you to watch for me, didn't I? Come along. We've little time."

"Come where? Time for what?"

"Why to your tent, of course, to put on your armor."

Terence gaped. "Are you daft?"

"Come and see."

Bemused, Terence followed Robin to a silken tent set up in the visitors' section. Inside he found a brilliant suit of armor, shining like gold, such as he had never seen in his life. His eyes lit with admiration. "By heaven!" he murmured. "Whose...?"

"Yours, your grace. Come now, the jousting will be over soon."

"Do you mean...? Robin, you *are* dotty! I'm not going to go jousting."

"Don't you wish to defend the honor of Avalon?"

"Less of it, Robin! What does Avalon care about a child's game like a tournament joust? Tell me what's up."

Robin shrugged. "I couldn't say. I only do what I'm told." He paused and added, "Do you?"

Terence frowned. "But I can't joust! You know that!"

"I know nothing of the sort. You've received tilting instruction from the greatest of all of this world's knights."

"Yes, but Gawain—"

"I didn't mean Gawain."

Terence frowned, uncomprehending. Then he understood. "Arthur," he whispered. Robin began lacing the golden armor onto Terence while Terence tried furiously to remember the instructions that Arthur had given him so long ago, after he had defeated Terence so ingloriously in Terence's only other real joust.

The trumpeters were preparing to announce the end of the lists when Terence, astride a magnificent bay stallion, rode to the edge of the tilting yard. Terence barely had time to whisper "Don't use my real name!" before Robin rode ahead to the king's pavilion to announce him.

"O king!" Robin declared. "I come as envoy from my master, this great knight you see before you!" He waved grandly at Terence.

Arthur nodded a greeting, saying, "And has your master a name, friend page?"

Robin smiled broadly. "Of course, sire. I present to you...Sir Wozzell!"

Terence sighed. Beside the king, Eileen started violently. She peered closely at Robin, then at Terence.

"You and your master are welcome," Arthur replied mildly. "May I serve you?"

"We have come to try our mettle against your greatest knights. I hope we have not come too late."

"Indeed, friend," Arthur said, "we were about to crown our champion, Sir Lancelot."

"Then would your champion consent to a challenge?" Robin asked immediately. "One pass to determine the greatest knight in England?"

Sir Lancelot, standing nearby and listening to the exchange, immediately declared, "My liege, if you would approve, I accept Sir Wozzell's challenge!"

Arthur nodded. "So be it. I see your master has no lance. Please tell him that he may choose a lance from our own stores."

"You are graciousness itself, O king," said Robin, bowing. He trotted back to Terence. "You heard all that, your grace?"

Terence nodded glumly. "Lancelot himself, eh? I wish you could tell me why I'm doing this. He'll break every bone I have, you know."

"Nay, it's not so bad," Robin said reassuringly. "Bones mend after time. Come on. Let's choose a lance."

At the tent of the royal armorer, Terence surveyed the court's collection of gaily painted lances through the slits in his visor. He dared not show his face, lest he be recognized. Robin suggested a lance painted all in green, and the armorer urged Terence to use a particularly long one. Both looked unwieldy to Terence. Nearby, a little boy played knight, galloping on a stick horse and waving a miniature lance, about a third the length of a real one. "Is that your son?" Terence asked the armorer.

"Yes, sir."

Suddenly, Terence grinned. "And did you make that lance for him?"

"Yes, sir. It was a good stout lance, but I broke it by carelessness, so I made it into a toy."

"That's the one I want." The armorer and Robin stared, speechless, and Terence stepped up to the boy. "Excuse me, sir knight," he said. "I could not help noticing your lance. It seems a rare weapon. May I ask you a favor? Could I borrow your weapon to use in a joust against Sir Lancelot?" The boy smiled happily and handed over the lance. Terence raised his visor so that only the boy could see his face and winked at him.

The armorer and Robin, in turns, expostulated and tried to dissuade Terence, but all Terence would say was "Didn't I say that a tournament joust was a child's game?"

Soon Terence sat on his mount at one end of the lists, facing Sir Lancelot across the tilting yard. Gawain had joined Eileen in the king's pavilion, and they were watching the strange Sir Wozzell intently. The court rippled with amazed laughter at Terence's lance, and more than one knight called for the king to disqualify the impudent challenger who so mocked the noble institution of knighthood. Arthur only looked amused and called for the joust to begin.

The trumpet sounded, and Sir Lancelot spurred his horse into a dead run. Terence gently urged his own horse into a gentle trot; what he meant to do would be easier at a slower pace. Sir Lancelot neared, his lance aimed straight at Terence's breastplate, his body leaning forward against the expected impact. But then Terence stopped his horse, swiftly reversed the child's lance so that he held it by the tapered end. With a sharp blow, Terence parried the point of the approaching lance, then swung the heavy end of the lance as if it were a cudgel. The dull thud of Terence's club on Sir Lancelot's helmet sounded like an axe on a log. Sir Lancelot flipped neatly over his horse's hindquarters and fell heavily into the dirt.

All the court was shocked and silent. Terence tossed his lance to Robin. "Take this back to that boy, will you?" he said.

Then all the court exploded with noise. A few, like Gawain and Sir Kai roared with laughter, several cheered, but many more shouted angrily that the stranger knight had behaved dishonorably. At last the king stood and raised his hand for silence as Terence trotted up to the royal pavilion. "Sir Wozzell," Arthur said, "I declare you the winner!" A few knights protested again, but Arthur said sharply, "I know of no rule against such bravery! Would any of you have dared to face Sir Lancelot with a ... a child's toy lance?" In the ensuing hush, Arthur turned back to Terence. "I must admit, though, that I found your methods unorthodox."

Terence spoke quietly. "The best fighter is not the

one who does the expected most skillfully. The best fighter is the one who takes the rest by surprise."

Arthur looked sharply at Terence; then his face cleared as enlightenment dawned, and a broad grin split his face. "Well spoken, my friend! I award you this necklace, the prize for the winner. It is yours to keep or to give away as you wish."

It was the moment when the winner of a tournament usually gave his prize to the lady of his choice. Terence looked toward Eileen, but then caught sight of Queen Guinevere. Since the joust, the queen had done nothing but stare at Sir Lancelot, now sitting up groggily in the mud. Her eyes looked empty and even frightened, like the eyes of a lost child. Terence's heart went out to her.

"Wait!" a voice called from behind Terence. Holding his dented helm in one hand, Sir Lancelot staggered forward. "My king, I beg you. Is there no way that this decision can be set aside?"

"No, Sir Lancelot. Sir Wozzell has won the day, and has earned the name of The Greatest Knight in England."

Sir Lancelot gave a deep moan. "Then I crave your permission to go away to bury my shame. I shall become a hermit, deep in the woods, living on roots and allowing myself to see no mortal man—"

"Oh, for heaven's sake, Lance," the queen interrupted, with surprising vehemence. "Don't listen to him, Arthur. He's always saying stuff like that. 'Give me that rose from your gown or I'll go die in a hermitage' 'Say you'll dance with me or I'll eat dirt.' It doesn't mean a thing. Just ignore him."

Sir Lancelot's mouth opened wide. "But Peerless Perfection of—"

"Shut up! Don't call me that! I have a name, you know!"

Sir Lancelot moaned again, and sat in the dirt, staring at Guinevere in amazement. Gawain looked down and began to shake quietly. Arthur's lips quivered, but his voice was grave when he said, "Again, O knight, I present this necklace to you."

"No, O king," Terence said as loudly as he could. "I cannot accept this prize, and I am not the Greatest Knight in England. In all my vast experience as a knight—" Terence could not help grinning and was glad that the visor hid his face—"I have been unhorsed only once. And the knight who so soundly defeated me is here present. I return this prize to you, King Arthur, in honor of the time when you struck me down. Do you remember?"

King Arthur's eyes twinkled, and he said, "I remember, Sir...Sir Wozzell. And I accept your tribute." He turned to his Queen. "Guinevere, my love, will you accept this prize from my hand?"

Guinevere smiled timidly and nodded, and Arthur placed the chain around his queen's neck.

Then, tentatively, she reached out to the king, and Arthur pulled her to his breast and held her in a long embrace. All the court watched the king and queen, some with delight, some with consternation. Gawain grinned happily at his friend, and said quietly, "You can't have too many Sir Wozzells."

For her part, Eileen gazed with adoration at her knight, the Duke of Avalon, and silently mouthed the words, "Well done, my love."

Author's Note

When I was in college during medieval times, about 1982, Dr. Laura Crouch required my English literature class to read a poem called *Sir Gawain and the Green Knight*. It was the most wonderful story I had ever encountered. I loved its brave and courteous hero, and I was fascinated by the otherworldly scene at the Green Chapel. I loved the poem so much that I wrote a long and very complicated research paper on it, and like many of those who write about literature, I managed to footnote away all the poem's charm and to make *Sir Gawain and the Green Knight* seem as dull and pretentious as I was.

Well, I did no irreparable damage. My paper is long forgotten, but the poem is still around. All the same, some of the things I learned while researching that paper are still interesting to me and may be to others. So, at the risk of being boring twice on the same subject (an unforgivable sin), here is some background to the original work on which this book is based.

Sir Gawain and the Green Knight was written by an anonymous poet in the fourteenth century, at about the same time that the great English poet Geoffrey Chaucer was writing *The Canterbury Tales*. The Gawain poet, however, wrote in a completely different dialect of English than Chaucer.

Although *Sir Gawain and the Green Knight* is one of the oldest known Arthurian works, the story of the tit-for-tat beheading game is older still. Similar stories are told of other heroes. For instance, an old Irish story called *Bricriu's Feast* relates the tale of an Irish hero, Cucholinn (or Cuchulainn, or Cuchulain), who faced a test like Gawain's. Evidently, the Gawain poet adapted an old story to fit a new hero.

That's how things go with heroes, it seems, because a hundred years after *Sir Gawain and the Green Knight* was written, Gawain was no longer considered the greatest knight of all. King Arthur's tales were being told by French poets, and in their stories the greatest knight in the English court was an imported French chap named Lancelot du Lac. Gawain was still around in the French stories, but he was portrayed as a rude and blustering fellow with few morals and even fewer manners.

This is all nonsense, of course. To those of us who have met the courageous, courteous, and humble hero of *Sir Gawain and the Green Knight,* Gawain will always be the perfect knight. Still, when I retold the story of Gawain's greatest quest, I purposely set it during a transitional time, when Lancelot's star was on the rise. By writing about different eras of Arthurian legend, I was able to adopt details and characters from other Arthurian stories. For example, I took the battle with the Emperor of Rome from *Le Morte D'Arthur,* by Sir Thomas Malory, and I've borrowed some of my minor characters from *Parzival,* by Wolfram von Eschenbach. And some of the people and events of this book are my own inventions — most notably the characters of my hero and heroine, Terence and Eileen.

After all, one can't have too many heroes.